PSY TOUCH

by A. D. McLain

To my husband. Thank you for helping me focus on one project when my mind was bouncing around to four. I couldn't have done it without your support and encouragement.

1

In her dreams, she had a family. Her mother and father laughed and smiled while watching the grandchildren playing in the backyard. A small boy would run and climb the ladder to the slide. A young girl sat on the swing, going higher and higher until she finally jumped out, a giggling cannonball, and splashed into a pile of leaves. She would stand and sprint back to the swing to do it again. Sunlight reflected red highlights off her sandy colored curls. The smell of rich Sunday cooking filled the house. Freshly baked ham and an assortment of sides were lined out on the counter. The oven timer rang, and her mother pulled out the pecan pie to let it cool. Lexy would lean against her husband and feel him wrap his arms around her while resting his chin on her head. She could never see his face, and whenever she attempted to, the dream would end, so she stopped trying. This was enough.

Her father would go to the backdoor after giving her mom a quick kiss and stealing a cookie from the cooling rack. He called out to the boy and girl, and they dashed inside to eat.

"Mommy." The boy would grab Lexy around the legs and squeeze.

She patted his head and told him to follow his sister and go wash up.

"Yes, Mom." They would climb the step stool by the sink.

"This is perfect," Lexy said.

"Yes, it is," a deep voice said, from behind her.

She turned and her mouth was captured in a hard, passionate kiss.

This was perfect. And for these few moments, it was all hers.

THE VIBRATION of her phone against the nightstand woke Lexy. She stretched and her sleeve got caught on the metal band around her head, pulling it across her forehead. Cringing, she resisted the urge to rip off the band, and gently disengaged the fabric. She swung her legs over the side of the bed, hurried to the bathroom and slammed the door shut. A drop of blood dripped onto the white tile at her feet. She looked at her reflection and saw a rivulet of blood snaking from the cut just below her hairline.

After grabbing the band with both hands, she pressed the disengage buttons and slipped it away from her head. The moment it was free from her skin and hair, she clenched it and resisted the desire to break it.

It was regulated to keep a minimum of two at all times, but the spare was in a box in her closet. She couldn't get to it without leaving the bathroom, and she couldn't leave the bathroom without her band on. This was the only crystaled room in her apartment. She couldn't afford to have any others done, and without the protection of the crystals or her inhibitor band, she would be at the mercy of any Psy pulses in the area. Even through the crystals she could sense the subtle vibrations and dim lights from the other people in the building. She couldn't tell what they were doing, but she could get a sense of how many people there were and where they were.

After taking a cotton swab from the drawer, she cleaned the cut, then applied disinfectant and a liquid bandage. A regular bandage would only get caught on her band and cause it to sit awkwardly on her head. As she dabbed the cut, she noticed the green specks in her otherwise blue eyes and was transported back to the dream. She had her father's eyes. That and her Psy power were all she had left of him. How she wished she could live a life like the one she dreamed. At one time, not that long ago, people did live like that. Her parents told her stories about their lives growing up, and at work she read similar stories from that time period. That was before the Storm.

After the Great Psy Storm of the early twenty-first century, everything changed. If you thought about touching someone, they felt it and the contact was as real as a physical touch. The Psy-sex industry exploded. You could be pleasured by thoughts and you didn't need to have physical intercourse to feel it. STD's dropped to nearly zero. Divorces skyrocketed. So did arrests. After all, pleasant thoughts weren't the only things that could be shared. You could strangle a person with a thought. Some killers got creative, causing blood clots or slowly suffocating a person by gradually increasing pressure on the lungs. Society shattered into a debauchery-filled experience of exploration with no rules.

Then came the over-correct after people realized all Psy all the time wasn't good. No one procreated or concentrated on work, and many people developed nervous disorders from a constant fear of being psychically violated or killed. So scientists developed inhibitor headbands to block the Psy pulse. While wearing a band, you couldn't influence others or be influenced by them.

Due to fear of the brutal impulses carried out by many, all books and movies were stripped of violence. The news was forbidden from reporting anything violent. The theory was, if people didn't see it, they wouldn't think violent thoughts. But it didn't work. It only meant the public was ignorant that the crime rate remained as high as before, so they felt safer and began living in a naive bubble. Detractors were arrested and removed before they could upset others. Free zones were established, where people could go to remove their bands. Society split into four factions—the Psy addicts, who lived in Psy dens and hardly ever wore the bands. Natripsyless, who never took the bands off. Recreational Psy users, who lived in-between those two extremes. And Prosers, who used their Psy abilities for professional purposes like massage or psychic surgery. Some people claimed there was a fifth group known as Pure Psys or Unchained, who'd learned to live band-less without becoming Psy addicts. No one knew if they existed.

Lexy fell into the Natripsyless group. She never removed her band in public, and rarely in private. There was another name for a Natripsyless—Psudes, or psychic prudes. With most sexual contact occurring psychically, it was common for most Natripsyless to be virgins, and psychic virgins were distrusted. It was viewed as unnatural.

A knock came at Lexy's bedroom door.

"Are you ready?" her roommate, Kara, called.

"In a minute." Lexy pulled on the closest work shirt and pants and stepped into her shoes.

After brushing her long brown hair in a handful of quick strokes, she replaced her band, wiped the blood from the floor, and then opened the door.

"It's about time." Kara tapped her toes, arms crossed as she leaned back against the kitchen counter. "We're going to be late."

"Since when do you care?" Lexy picked up her purse and followed Kara to the car. "You're always late."

"Not this month. I haven't been late once in the past three weeks."

"Ah." Lexy settled into the passenger seat of Kara's car.

Now she understood. Their employer, History Remembered, had incentive programs in place to encourage punctuality and high performance. If an employee was on time four weeks in a row, they would be rewarded with an extra Psy session. Everyone was allowed one session per day, and all staff was permitted to remove their inhibitor bands for thirty minutes prior to lunch or at the end of the workday. Employees from the HR department would send out pleasure thoughts to everyone during these periods. Nearly every company offered this incentive, believing that at least one psygasm a day led to healthier, happier people. It relieved tension and stress, fostered comradery between co-workers, and led to a decrease in absenteeism and tardiness.

History Remembered, a federally run, national document analysis and preservation company, was unique in that it offered extra sessions as a reward for achievement. The faster you completed your projects, the more you could earn. If you were an active participant in the state's Healthy Living Initiative, which tracked exercise, steps walked in a day, calories consumed while away from work, dental hygiene habits, and other health-related decisions, you could earn one new session a month. Now, companies weren't sought for how many vacation days you could earn. Instead, employees wanted to earn pleasure they could enjoy at the office. Many employees even voluntarily worked weekends at their regular rate instead of insisting on overtime pay, just to get more sessions. Of course, the heavy club-goers didn't care. They could find a way to Psy-play no matter where they were.

Kara turned into the on-ramp lane and let the car take over driving. Their daily lesson began playing over the radio. Most main roads were wired to electronically control vehicles, supposedly to increase safety and decrease road rage. Cars were automatically re-routed around break-downs or flat tires, and you couldn't get lost. Most side roads and driveways weren't wired, but there was minimal driving required to get to one that was. Even for those with long commutes, few people drove more than a few minutes every day.

Kara flipped the radio from lesson to music. Every car had a handful of listening options. If you listened to at least one lesson every other day, you could earn more Healthy Living Points—HLPs. Listen to one or more lessons a day and you earned double points for the week. But the lessons were monotone and boring. Kara would only go so far for free psygasms. Lexy was relieved at that, since they had to carpool because only one parking spot was allowed at work for the both of them.

"How many sessions have you accrued now, anyway?" Kara flipped through the available three music stations and settled on one that played festive multicultural music from around the world.

"Ten, I think. Not sure. Maybe fifteen."

"You should use one, or at least try and see if you can transfer any to me." Kara grinned.

"I'd transfer all of them to you if I could. You know I don't care about any of that."

The sky was clear blue. Distant streaks of orange and red indicated the recent sunrise now hidden behind the mountains on the horizon. People in the surrounding cars stared straight forward, chatted with their car mates, or leaned back with their eyes closed. No one was looking at the horizon.

"I know," Kara said. "I just don't see why you sit out every day. It's no big deal."

"Not my thing. I'd rather spend the time getting extra work done."

The car alarm beeped three times to signal their exit from

the wired road. They came to a stop in line behind three other vehicles. Kara pressed the button to take back control over of the car and pulled out at the change of the light. Following the other cars, she drove into the parking garage and then pulled into their spot. Kara jogged up the steps to the building and hopped for joy when the time clock blinked green as she passed her card through. It blinked red if you were late or leaving early.

"Catch you at lunch." Kara waved and strode down the hall, to her office.

Lexy shook her head and slid her own card through the time clock. Her light blinked red.

"Oh, well."

She passed through the break room full of boisterous people discussing weekend plans and some television show from the previous night. They were all laughing, filling their coffee cups, and preparing for the day. Lexy went straight to her office without talking to anyone. The breakfast cart would come by soon, so she wasn't worried about getting anything to drink right then.

After hovering her card in front of the door with her name, she heard the soft click of the lock releasing. Her office was dark and quiet, just the way she liked it. She hit the play button on her music player and the office was filled with classical music. She squirted a few drops of aromatherapy oil into her air purifier and dimmed the lights. The harsh white light from the other setting hurt her eyes when she tried to read. She was halfway into her third book of the morning when the breakfast cart came around.

Back in the days when Psy violence was common, many studies were done to determine what contributed to feelings of anger and depression. Improper food choices due to lack of healthy eating options was found to be a contributing factor. Therefore, many bad foods were banned, but the government still couldn't control what a person ate at home. They couldn't force people to eat enough of the required nutrients. At first, they tried requiring daily multi-vitamins, but it didn't translate to a substantial change in happiness levels. So they came up with the workplace food initiative. Employers were provided with guidelines for healthy meal options for three meals a day. Workdays were extended to allot the time needed to eat those extra meals. People were then allowed to eat however they chose after work hours and on off-days, but they still weren't allowed to purchase unhealthy food items, except in small quantities and for special occasions. Everyone was allowed three desert passes per year to redeem for the treat of his or her choice. You placed your request a month prior to redemption and the desert was delivered to your home on the day requested.

Just as Lexy was finishing her breakfast sandwich, she heard the bell ring, signaling for everyone to come to the break room. She sighed, wondering what it would be this time. The pile of paperwork on her desk stared back at her and there was still a lot of scanning left to do. She ejected and pocketed her memory card, then got up. The legs of her chair scraped across the floor as she pushed back. Once outside her office, she drifted behind the rest of the crowd.

"Attention, everyone," one of the managers on her floor called.

She couldn't remember his name. Jim or Tim, maybe. Something short.

"We have a birthday today. Everyone take off your bands for Natalie from accounting.

Everyone except Lexy removed their inhibitor bands and stared, smiling at the woman standing in the center of the room. Her breathing sped up. Her face became flushed. She stumbled into the seat beside her. Painted, manicured nails clung to the arm of the chair and she struggled to keep standing. Finally, she moaned and stopped shaking. Everyone put back on their bands back on and clapped and cheered.

Natalie beamed and held up a hand. "Thank you, everyone. That was great."

The manager cut into a cake on the counter and began handing out thin slices to be passed around the room. That was one benefit of working in a large company. You were able to supplement your desert allotments with the occasional slice of birthday cake, though it was usually a health-conscious, low-fat version of some fruit or carrot cake. This one looked like a banana cake.

Lexy turned, ignoring the plate being held out for her, and went back to her office. The rest of the day went by without much incident. She spent her lunch hour swimming in the company pool. Eating in the cafeteria was always awkward after a birthday. Word inevitably got around that she hadn't participated in the group psygasm again. Everyone would whisper comments and shoot her looks when she walked by.

A group-stimulated psygasm was a rare, coveted treat, unless you frequented some of the racier Psy dens, and it was considered rude not to contribute your pulse. But the negative responses lessened every year, since she refused her own birthday psygasms. People didn't get as angry at her skipping out on their gift if she wasn't accepting pulse back from them on her day. The resentment they once directed at her was mostly gone now, replaced by curiosity and confusion. She was weird and shy, but no one thought she was selfish.

The bell rang for the end of the workday. Thankful the day was over, Lexy sat back and stretched before heading down to the car, where she waited. Clicking through her watch, she checked her bank account balance, played a puzzle game, and counted the cracks in the brick wall in front of her. She checked her watch and looked out the car window again. Kara stumbled down the steps by the doorway and rushed to the car. She jumped into the driver's side.

"Sorry." She panted and was flushed. "I got an extra Psy session for finishing my work on the census transcriptions project."

"Not a problem. Let's just get home."

The noise in the parking garage grew louder as more people filed out and got in their cars to leave.

"Didn't I tell you?" Kara backed out and headed to the waiting ramp for the wired road, a dance mix playing on the radio. "We're going out tonight." She tapped her fingers along the steering wheel, in time to the music.

Lexy leaned her head against the window, which had been chilled from the blasting air conditioner. That combined with the muggy heat from outside caused the window to fog briefly. She reached up and drew a swirl with her finger. Then it disappeared.

"I really don't feel like it."

"You have to. We're going to meet up with Ben, Trae, and Wendy at the concert hall."

"I don't even know them."

Kara frequently went out with them to the clubs on weekends.

"Sure you do. We work with them every day."

"You work with them every day. I work alone, and I don't go to the Psy session lounge with the rest of you."

Kara blinked and shook her head. "Well, you should, if for no other reason than to talk to other people every now and then. They're great guys. You just need to give them a chance. Besides, the concert will be fun, and Ben said his friend Curtis is coming, and he's bringing another male friend along." She winked. "So there'll be someone there for each of us."

"I don't know. I don't have much luck with dating and I'm not into hookups."

"All the more reason to come. You've got to learn to let go and relax, before you have a Psy-fit or something." Kara took back control of the car.

Lexy stiffened. Being accused of emotional instability or a propensity for Psy violence was no easy threat. She didn't think Kara meant anything by it, and she knew Kara wasn't likely to turn her in, but it still wasn't a good sign. Lexy tried to keep her head low and be as unobtrusive as possible, but maybe she wasn't doing a good enough job of it. How long before someone else looked at her lack of participation and came to the same conclusion? She'd have to start doing a better job of acting normal and non-threatening.

"I'll come."

They got out of the car and walked up the stairs, to the door.

Kara was beaming.

"Just give me ten minutes to get ready and I'll meet you out front. But I'm taking my own car, so that I can leave when I want."

"Not a problem. See you in ten."

2

J ared walked by the wall and tried to stay out of the way. The room was already getting crowded.

"Over here," Curtis called, from a set of couches over to one side.

Ben and the others were already there. Jared recognized Ben and his date, Monique. She was a small girl with a bouncy, curly hairstyle and too much makeup. She always wore too much makeup and perfume. As he walked closer, he got a whiff of the wild oleander and jasmine fragrance she preferred. Beside them were two of Ben's friends from work and their dates. The friends had made an appearance or two at Curtis's parties. The dates were new.

"Are we ready to go in?" Jared asked.

"Not yet." Curtis sat on one of the couches and motioned for everyone else to do the same. "They haven't started seating the hall yet and we're still waiting on two people."

"Who?"

"Their names are Kara and Lexy," Ben said. "They're from my work."

Jared raised an eyebrow to Curtis and leaned in. "Is this some kind of blind date setup thing?" he whispered.

Curtis grinned. "Well, I met Kara at Ben's house a couple weeks ago," he whispered back. "When I mentioned the concert and told her who all was coming, she suggested bringing her roommate. So you're welcome."

Jared groaned. "You know I hate setups."

"It's just for the concert, so calm down. If you don't like her, you can pick up someone else later. Oh, look, there they are now."

Jared looked at the two women entering the lobby. They couldn't have been more different. One was dressed in a fiery-red and black asymmetrical dress with see-through cuts of black lace revealing her pale skin. Short black hair cut into a bob framed a made-up face with bright red lipstick and dramatic black lined eyes. The other woman was dressed modestly, with free flowing blond hair and simple white flats. She seemed much less comfortable being here.

The first woman smiled and waved at Curtis. The second woman fell back, distracted by an elderly woman with a walker, trying to get through the door. Around them, people pushed past, aggravated at the obstacle in their path. Some pushed the old woman or rolled their eyes. A group of high school kids jammed into the small opening beside her and shoved her into the door frame. Her purse fell to the ground, items spilling in all directions to be trampled by oblivious or uncaring concert goers.

"Lexy, come on," Kara called back, stopping halfway between the door and the couches.

Lexy shot Kara an aggravated look and held open the door for the woman to get through. Then she bent over and retrieved all the items that'd fallen from her purse. A couple people stepped on her hands or hit her in the head with their bags, but she didn't yell at them or complain. She simply filled the purse for the old lady and handed it back to her. The woman took Lexy into a strong hug and thanked her for her help. Lexy bit her lip, looked off to the side and mumbled something Jared couldn't hear over the crowd. Then she strolled over in their direction.

"Hey, Lexy," Kara said, as soon as she was within hearing distance.

Jared looked over, startled. He hadn't noticed when Kara reached them. She sat next to Curtis, and the two of them were holding hands and casting flirty smiles at each other.

"Can you grab us all a drink?" Kara said.

Lexy opened her mouth, then closed it and smiled. "Sure."

After glancing at the group to count how many heads there were, she headed to the bar.

"Is she my date?" Jared asked.

Maybe this night wouldn't be as bad as he thought. She wasn't like the others.

"Good luck with her," Trae said. "She's a Pseude."

"What?" Curtis darted his gaze away from Kara, which was saying something because the two of them were practically joined at the pulse, even with the bands on. "Are you serious? Is she, like, some kind of Natripsyless? Only likes *real* sex?"

Everyone cringed. Physical intercourse was looked down on. It was messy, disease-ridden. You had to take your clothes off, and you always risked producing offspring. There were some die-hards who still claimed it was the only way to go, but most people didn't see the point. It may have its benefits, but why would anyone give up the responsibility-free lifestyle of no-strings psinterludes with hundreds of partners for thirty minutes to an hour of risky physical copulation?

For those who still wanted to have children, there was always the traditional route or state-sponsored surrogates. Most people, even those in committed relationships, went with the surrogate route. Financially, it made the most sense. The government dissolved the institute of marriage a decade after the Storm. With a divorce rate near eighty percent, domestic violence at a historical high, and more people opting for the commitment-free lifestyle that their new abilities offered them, all state-sanctioned marriages were halted. Churches could hold their own marriage ceremonies for couples who wished to participate, but the government no longer treated a married couple any different than an unmarried couple. Their assets and tax reporting weren't joined. They could come or go from the relationship without filing any paperwork or fearing child and spousal support rulings. Women no longer legally changed their name, and their children could take either name.

A major uproar developed over the validity of Psy-sex as a reason for divorce. Was it really cheating if they never physically touched another person? Prenuptial agreements with adultery clauses were hotly contested in court and on television. Anger over these and other normal marital problems led to many Psy attacks and killings, accidental and intentional. Your spouse could kill you in your sleep, while they were only half-awake. This was before the inhibitor bands became mandatory in all zones except free ones.

But that led to a significant population drop. While many people lauded the change, citing population overgrowth concerns from the past, the fact remained that society needed children to keep going. As people grew sick and died, they needed to be replaced. Jobs went unfilled, services were canceled, and businesses went under. So the government stepped in again, setting up incentive programs to encourage people to have children. Women began opting for anonymous insemination, at the direction of the state. All maternity-related medical bills and other expenses were covered during the first two years of infancy. After that, the woman could opt to keep the child or enroll them in early preschool houses which saw to their continued care and development. Then the woman could go back to her life or opt to have another child.

The consequence of this program was far-reaching. Couples were encouraged to opt for anonymous insemination instead of traditional procreation to secure maternity and infant financial support from the state. Couples who chose to produce their own children through physical intercourse weren't eligible for this compensation and were required to provide for their own medical and financial needs. Mothers, even ones who opted to continue having children, rarely kept their children past the age of two, since that was when state support ceased, and they were required to take over the financial burden of the child.

Of course, none of this stopped people from dating. Some people still sought out long-term relationships, just without the commitment level seen in past generations. There was a huge shift in attitudes from the time before the Storm.

Jared brought his mind back to the present and wished he hadn't. A couple guys in the group were mimicking real sex, to the enjoyment of the others. Everyone was laughing and joining in, calling out exclamations about enjoying having to stop what they were doing to put on contraceptive protection and take off their clothes in the middle of a cold room. Curtis and Kara were laughing right along with the rest of them.

Jared caught movement from his peripheral and saw Lexy standing ten feet away. She was looking down, and he could tell by the pull of her brow and tensed muscles that she knew how this conversation had started. Then she took a breath. Her shoulders relaxed and her face rose into a bright smile.

"Got the drinks." She strode up to the couches.

The others snickered and tried not to laugh as they took their glasses from the tray she carried. Lexy ignored them and continued to smile.

Jared took his glass and looked up at her, with sincerity. "Thank you."

Her gaze flicked over to his, and he felt his awareness expand. While clamping down on his emotions, he noticed her expression was drawn inward. She set down the tray and took a seat on an empty chair, distancing herself from the group. They hardly noticed. Her roommate threw a few comments her way, but for the most part, they left her alone.

She scooped up an orange from the fruit basket on the end-table beside her and picked at the skin with unpainted nails. Her face was barely made-up, too. A light gloss the same color as her lips disappeared after the first few bites, leaving her with faint eye shadow as her only adornment. She wore no jewelry except the inhibitor band around her head. He noticed a small scratch just below the band. It looked new. Beside it were older scratches and healed scars, a sure sign of someone who slept wearing a band. Those who could afford it opted for a crystal post bed. Those who couldn't had to sleep in the band, or go without and hope they weren't caught. Few people had the will power to keep up long-term night-wear without sneaking in a few band-less nights.

Lexy pushed back a stray lock of hair and brushed against the scratch. Screwed her face up at the unexpected contact but didn't say anything. She wore a simple, straight-cut dress that fell just below her knees and only moderately showed her curves. The sleeveless top covered her cleavage.

As she tapped her foot in time with the music in the background, he couldn't help but feel like it was all a show. The way she presented herself was completely thought out. It was simple enough not to attract too much attention, reserved enough to preserve her modesty, but flirty enough not to make her seem like a Psude. The overall effect was a nice girl who may be shy. Perhaps that was what she was and it wasn't a disguise. He doubted it.

The music in the concert hall picked up, signaling the start of the show. Everyone stood and pressed through the thick crowd. Curtis and Kara took the lead. Lexy fell to the back, letting the others push in front of her. Jared fell back enough to keep an eye on her. While entering the concert hall, he saw the group take their seats, leaving only one empty spot beside them. Curtis waved back at Jared to take the seat. Behind him, Lexy furtively glanced around for somewhere to go. Resignation and acceptance shone on her face. Jared looked once more at his friend, who was now too distracted by Kara to worry about Jared. So he grabbed his opening, went to Lexy and took her hand.

She looked at him, brow raised. "What are you—"

"Follow me." He led her back out into the lobby and down another hall.

"Where are we going?"

"You'll see." Jared pushed aside a black curtain to reveal a set of hidden stairs.

Lexy looked at him, biting the corner of her mouth. Then she relaxed and smiled. Followed him up the stairs, to a service balcony overlooking the entire hall. After pulling a loose tarp from the corner, he spread it out for them to sit on and they settled in for the start of the concert.

"How did you know about this place?" she whispered.

"Summer job when I was younger."

"What about your friend? Won't he miss you?"

"I doubt it. I tend to do my own thing. He's used to it."

"That sounds nice."

"I'm Jared, by the way."

"Lexy." She offered her hand, then settled back into a more comfortable position.

Jared shifted beside her and took in the lighting as it reflected off the ceiling. Orange and green stage lights moved across the room, changing color where they crossed. Leaning back against the wall, he reached up and disengaged his inhibitor band, then carefully removed it.

She took a sharp breath, eyes wide. "What are you doing?" A look of real fear crossed her face. She glanced back down the stairs.

"Relax. No one can see up here and there aren't any cameras. You can take yours off if you like."

"I... no, I can't." Her body shook and she scooted a few inches back.

"It's all right. No pressure. Look, would you feel better if I put mine back on?"

She gazed over at him, nibbling her lip. He put on the band back on.

She sighed. "I'm sorry."

"Don't worry about it. It's fine. I won't do it again. Now lean back and try to relax."

She scooted beside him and touched her shoulder to his. He waited a few songs, until she was smiling again, before putting his arm around her. She settled back against him and rested her head against his chest, straightening her legs and crossing her ankles. Their fingers were intertwined. He closed his eyes, listening to the music, and let his heartbeat and breathing slow to match hers.

The music rose and fell, with the crowd cheering when the more popular songs were played. Lexy smiled and mouthed the words. She tapped her toes and moved her head with the beat.

"So tell me, what's your path?" he asked, during a slow song.

Everyone chose or was placed in a certain career path based on their skills. It wasn't a decision to be taken lightly, and some-one's path could tell you a lot about them. When the popula-tion dropped, certain jobs took priority. Positions needed to keep society going. You couldn't have hundreds of thousands of people studying art or music theory when you needed doctors or welders. So the universities began restructuring their programs, only offering degrees in useful professions and accepting a predetermined number of people into each degree program. Once you were placed on a certain path, it became difficult to jump to another. Every spot had to be filled, and it was all based on algorithms and formulas designed by bureaucrats and statisticians. If a city needed a certain number of plumbers based on its population and you wanted to leave that program, another student must first take your place. The only exception was if you wished to move into a job that had an optimal operating deficit. In some cases, people were *asked* to relocate to other areas or states to fill these deficits.

"I'm a data preservation specialist," she said.

"Data preservation? Isn't that secretive work?"

She nodded. "It puts me in contact with a lot of unapproved texts and content. After I transcribe, scan, or catalogue it, every piece is passed on to analysts to determine if the item will be censored or released to the public. Either way, I have to read it as I work."

"I've heard it can be a lonely job."

"I enjoy it. I like reading about people's thoughts and experiences, seeing the world through other's eyes. I've read love letters, wedding announcements, obituaries. Stories of tragedy and miraculous rescues. I've seen pictures of lovers separated by war, and children reunited with parents or siblings. Every day, I learn something new. Sometimes I think I have more in common with the people in those letters than I do with my coworkers and friends. They really saw the world differently back then." She sighed. "What about you?"

"On paper, I work for my dad. In truth, I've had dozens of unpaid apprenticeships in things like mechanics, wood and metal working. Electrical, hydroponics, and traditional agriculture."

"Preparing for the apocalypse?" She grinned.

"Some would say we're already there." He returned her grin. "I just don't like being told what to do or what I'm allowed to learn. If I want to learn something new, I go out and do it. As long as I don't get paid for it and don't stop doing my day job, there isn't anything they can say or do about it. So what's the most interesting thing you've ever read?"

"Hmmm, well, there was this one story about a man and his family. They were starving, stranded by a bad winter storm. They lived in a small mountain valley and were often wintered in when the pass was blocked by snow. But this year, their main home and all their food was destroyed by a fire, early into their stay. Every day, the man went out in freezing temperatures, without adequate clothing to keep him warm. He searched for anything for his family to eat, setting traps, rummaging nuts, and pulling fish from an ice cold stream with only a staff with a knife tied onto the end. Despite his efforts, there wasn't enough food for everyone to eat, so every night he would take a single bite of fish and give the rest to his wife and children. He never complained, and he prayed every day to thank God for giving him even that much to eat. This went on for two months, until the mountain pass thawed, and they were able to make their way out. They were all sick from the ordeal, but they lived. Doctors who examined the man couldn't believe he'd survived on so little food for such a long period of time. They said it shouldn't have been possible. His family needed him, and he kept them alive. That would have to be the best story I've ever read."

Jared stared at her face in wonder, knowing this woman would be significant in his life. He wasn't sure yet if they'd be lovers, though it felt likely, but he knew she would be important to him.

They sat in silence for a while, listening to the concert and enjoying each other's company. When the music finally ended, they reluctantly stood and ambled back down the stairs. They stopped just before the curtain. The sounds of patrons filing out into the hall were all around them, and this was the last moment they'd have alone.

"I'd like to see you again," he said, in the darkened stairwell.

"Me, too." She pressed her hands against his, their fingers joining.

Jared resisted the urge to kiss her.

He took a deep breath. "There's an old skater's park down near the walking path into the woods. Can you meet me there tomorrow at lunch?"

"I'll be there." She closed her eyes.

For a moment, he let his control slip and psychically touched her cheek. She jolted her eyes open.

"Where'd they go?" Kara's asked, from outside the curtain.

"They've got to be around here somewhere," Curtis replied.

Jared smiled to Lexy. He was more than grateful for the interruption.

"You ready?"

She nodded and he pulled back the curtain.

Kara shrieked. "Where... where've you been? What were you doing back there?"

Lexy blushed.

"Hey," Jared said, "you all want to hit that diner down on Charles Street?"

Everyone began chatting about favorite foods at that diner and how good an iced drink would be at combating the muggy summer heat. Lexy and Jared's appearance from behind the curtain was forgotten.

With a hand at her back, Jared led Lexy to her car. "You coming?"

She looked over at the others, who were laughing as they loaded into their cars. "Not tonight, but I'll see you tomorrow."

"Can I get your profile?"

"Sure." Lexy lifted her arm and activated the touchscreen on her watch phone.

With a swipe, she pulled up her profile transfer settings. It was on moderate. The default options for any watch were anonymous, moderate, and full access. Anonymous gave only a first name and phone number. Full access transferred everything down to height, weight, birthdate, and grades in school. She pulled up the settings for moderate transfer and looked over everything, then clicked to allow age and email address. After a few seconds of indecision flitting over her features and a finger hovering over the checked box for physical address, she left it visible. After clicking to confirm, she held out her arm and let Jared touch his watch phone to hers. A click signaled the beginning of transfer. Then the lights on the sides of their screens turned red. A moment later, they heard a beep and the lights returned to green.

"Great," Jared said. "I transferred my info, too."

She looked down at his profile on her screen. "You live at Walnut Ridge?"

Jared tried not to let his unease show. "I know it's kind of a party area, but the rent is cheap and people tend to leave you alone."

She nodded. "I feel like I should warn you. What they all said about me is true. I never go Psy."

"I'll see you tomorrow."

She smiled. "See you then."

3

I t was chilly in Lexy's room. A glance at the thermometer on the clock by the bed showed why. The temperature was under seventy. Kara must've turned the air conditioner on after she got home, whenever that was. Lexy groaned and tapped the buttons on the screen to turn off the A/C. Hopefully it hadn't been on long enough to get their power shut off again.

If you used too much power in a given day, the electric company put wattage restrictions on your line which caused brown-outs or full-on power outages, depending on how far you went over. Same with the water. They had to relax all the low-flow toilet regulations after massive sewage backups destroyed the underground sewage network, and people never accepted the modified shower heads. Eventually, the government gave up trying to control water pressure and instead focused on overall usage. You could use an old-style, full-flow toilet or shower head, but you were only allotted so much water to use per day. After that, the water shut off and you had to wait until the next day to use it again. Now, people now were much more careful about when they used water, and living with a roommate made it worse. There was nothing more difficult than making amends after overusing the water and getting it shut off for everyone else. At work or in public, you had to swipe your watch in front of a faucet sensor to turn the water on or off. Depending on your job, you could be granted higher water allotments, but desk workers didn't qualify for much over the minimum.

Lexy groggily slipped her feet into her house shoes and padded to her door. Most mornings, she got dressed first. But this morning she needed something to drink or eat to perk her up. She lived in a small two-bedroom apartment with a shared living room and kitchen in the center of the bedrooms. Each bedroom had its own private bathroom, and the kitchen was open to the living room. Simple and convenient.

Lexy spent most of her time in her bedroom. Kara was considerate enough, as far as roommates went, but they had nothing in common. Sometimes Lexy longed for the chance to live alone or move back in with her mom. Better yet, she wanted a place that belonged to her. A place where she could raise a family and be free from all the constant interference from the outside world.

As she entered the living room, her desire to move out became even stronger. Kara and Curtis were on the sofa, rocking and moaning. They weren't wearing their inhibitor bands.

"Oh, come on!" Lexy said. "Can't you do that in your room?"

"Don't be a Psude," Kara said, between clenched teeth. "It's not like we're having sex. It's just—ahhh." She scrunched her face and squirmed in her seat. "It's just a little Psy-play." She gripped the couch, her face and neck growing red.

Across from her, Curtis was also breathing hard. And that wasn't the only thing that was hard. It was a good thing that men generally wore collection bags, or his nice slacks would've been ruined.

Before she could stop herself, Lexy wondered how many bags he'd already been through since last night. Then she shook her head and covered her eyes to avoid staring. They continued to moan and gyrate, not the least bit concerned about having an audience.

Lexy stomped to the kitchen to pour a glass of juice. Just then, papers and dishes fell from the coffee table. Curtis and Kara shook together, clutching onto the side of the table and the couch's fabric. Once they were done, they plopped back against the couch, with a shared sigh. Lexy rolled her eyes and went back to scavenging the cabinets for something to eat. After pulling out some bread and butter, she fired up the toaster and stepped back. Curtis said his goodbyes, put on his inhibitor band and left. Kara stumbled into the kitchen and filled a glass of water from the sink faucet. She downed it in one long gulp. The toaster dinged.

"So..." Lexy put another slice of bread in the toaster, "a simulgasm. I guess you two must be compatible."

Simultaneous psygasms were difficult to achieve, for two reasons. To stimulate another person psychically required concentration, which was hard to do while also being stimulated. Second, people were selfish, and a me-first mentality left little room for thinking about on someone else's pleasure. Usually the dominant person received the majority of the focus, returning the favor only as a means of asserting control over the other person.

"I like him." Kara shrugged. "What about you and his friend, Jared? How did your wavelengths mesh last night?"

"It wasn't like that. We just watched the concert like the rest of you."

"Speak for yourself." Kara put her glass down and took a slice of buttered toast from Lexy's plate. "Curtis and I disengaged the bands and started trading psygasms before the end of the third song. We didn't turn them back on until halfway through the last set. He has an incredible mind for pleasure. There was this one move he did—I swear I thought his mouth was actually on my breast, and the way he could stimulate multiple spots at the same time. Mmm. You should get him to loosen you up a bit. You could do a lot worse for your first psinterlude. I can ask him for you, if you want."

Lexy tried to restrain a look of discomfort and horror. "That's okay. Think I'll pass."

"Girl, you need to let go, already. I can help you get started, if that would be easier for you. I don't mind. It's at least an hour before I need to get to work."

Lexy choked on a piece of toast and took a swallow of juice. "Thanks, but no. I have a date with Jared today, anyway."

Kara grinned. "Oh, well in that case, have fun. Sure you don't need me to show you any tricks? There's this one where you imagine—"

"No!" Lexy threw her hands up. "Thank you. It's just a regular date."

"Aw, how cute. If you're feeling too shy, I can tag along and do him for you. He doesn't even have to know. He'll think it's you. That way you can ease into it, let him do his thing on you without all the stress of trying to focus on reciprocating. You can just enjoy. I'll just change my weekend workday to tomorrow. It'll be fine."

Kara really was trying to be helpful. In a way, it was kind of sweet. In a way.

Lexy closed her eyes and took a breath. "I appreciate the offer. I really do, but I'll be okay, I promise."

"Okay. But I expect a full report tonight."

"Sure. Oh, Kara, you know where my skates are? I spent an hour looking for them last night."

Kara cringed and dusted breadcrumbs from her hands. "Yeah, sorry about that. One of the wheels popped off the last time I wore them. I held on to them to get it fixed, but then I forgot about it. Why? Do you need them today?"

"I did. That's okay. Don't worry about it. I'll think of something else."

"No, wait." Kara rushed over to the tablet mounted on the wall and pulled up a shopping website. She found skates like the ones Lexy had. "Awesome, and they're on sale today, too. Here." She tapped the Buy-and-Print button on the screen, flipped the power switch on the printer and grinned. "According to the status bar, the skate should be finished printing in about thirty minutes. The other skate' is in my room."

Beside her, spinning and whirling sounds emanated from the 3D printer as the roller skate printed.

"Thanks. That gives me enough time to get dressed." Lexy turned to go back into her room.

Kara grabbed her arm. "Hey, check this out. They have the new shoes I wanted last week." She pointed to a black ballet shoe with a red dragon on the top and red trim along the side. "Those would look so awesome with the red shirt and black shorts I was planning to wear to work. They're on sale today, too. How cool is that? Wait, it has a three-hour download and print time? That sucks. That means I won't have them before I leave." Her face fell.

"No, but if you buy them now, they'll be ready for you by the time you get home. That way you can wear them out tonight."

Kara brightened again. "Yeah, I can wear them tonight. Curtis and I were planning on checking out that new nightclub on the edge of town. I can wear my red silk dress. Those shoes will be perfect with it."

Lexy left to get ready for her date.

* * *

SHE HELD her skates by the shoelaces, slung over her shoulder. The parking lot was full of cars, but there were few people around. A couple boys on skateboards did tricks up and down wooden ramps inside the concrete bowl thirty feet away. Lexy watched, captivated. They couldn't have been any more than thirteen or fourteen. They wore bands, or she would've guessed they were even younger.

"Look at this," one of them called out.

After gathering speed, he skateboarded up the side of the bowl and did a twisting jump off the edge. The trick was flawless, but his landing wasn't. He pulled his legs back around under him, but one wheel hit the ground at an angle, sending him off balance. At his neck, knees, and elbows, black pouch bands blossomed into an inflatable helmet and pads. He rolled across the ground and started laughing. His friend helped him to his feet and pushed the deflate button on the pouch around his neck. The inflatable protectors pulled back into the vinyl bags, again hidden from view.

"That was awesome," his friend said.

They went back to skating.

"Lexy, over here," someone called.

She turned and looked back over her car roof.

Jared walked over to her, smiling with a twinkle in his eyes. "You brought skates. Good."

He motioned to a bench and they sat to put their skates on.

"Want to leave your shoes in my car?" Lexy asked.

"No, we'll need them later. Come on."

Lexy took his hand and let him lead her down the walking path. A breeze blew as the sun beat down on them. She could feel small beads of sweat roll down her neck and back. Nut shells, empty and broken from previous walkers, crunched under their wheels. Sporadic trees became a forest with all the shade and relief afforded by their proximity. Without the constant sunlight, it became chilly.

"This way," Jared said, at a split in the path.

Lexy looked at the other passage. It turned and curved back toward the cars. The path they were now on stretched deeper into the forest.

The rolling trees were peaceful as the wind filtered through the branches, and Lexy felt her lids growing heavy. She clutched her fingers tighter around Jared's and felt a return squeeze. She grinned, wondering where this path could lead. Why would anyone create a paved pathway so deep into the woods? Flowers lined the passage, and limbs dangled above. Birds rustled leaves overhead. Squirrels scampered up tree trunks. A rabbit ducked under a bush. Perhaps the architects had wished to share this space with everyone so that even those on skateboards and roller skates could find rejuvenation in this alcove of natural treasures. With the skating bowl so near the walking path, she could imagine it met many travelers on wheels. Or perhaps it was designed by a hiker with limited time who wished to explore the woods more quickly. Without their skates, this walk would take substantially longer. But Lexy didn't care about that. She loved spending time outside, away from her apartment. But everyone she knew was always rushing. They rushed to work and rushed home so they could go out to the clubs. They rushed into and out of relationships, instead of sticking around to see how things could develop. Everything was centered on the moment.

Lexy looked at the uneven terrain and rocks peeking out of the ground. By contrast, the ground below the path was raised and smooth, to give an even walking surface. It was then that she realized the path was most likely put in to prevent falls while walking through the forest. Nature walks were generally looked upon highly. They had a calming effect on people and could lower stress. But when in nature, you were at greater risk of injury, and injuries caused negative thoughts and feelings. The path was a way to guide people and keep them safe. It was enough to make her want to take off her skates and go climb the farthest tree just to spite them.

"Here's a good place to stop." Jared brought them around to a tree stump wide enough for them both to sit. "Change into your shoes. We're going off-path."

"You must've read my mind." Lexy laughed silently to herself as she began unlacing her skates. "I was just thinking we should do that."

He chuckled. "No mind-reading here. We're going some-place specific, and you can't get there following the path any further."

He pulled off his skates and stuck his feet into pre-tied sneakers. They were soft and dingy. On the side, there were dark gray scuff marks, and the heel was bent in and cracking.

"Do you come out here a lot?" she asked.

"Sometimes. It's one of several places I go to relax. Here, hand me your skates." He held both of their skates by the laces and tied them to a low-hanging branch. "That way, they'll be here when we come back."

"What if someone takes them?"

"I leave stuff here all the time. It'll be fine. Besides, if I'm wrong, I'll buy you new ones."

With a wink, he took her hand and a shiver ran up her arm. They stood still for several moments, eyes locked, staring at each other. The wind blew and branches swayed. A beam of sunlight surrounded them, reflecting off white dandelion seeds swirling in the air.

"I don't know where you're planning on us going," Lexy said, "but I'd say this is a pretty good spot right here."

"Then you'll love what comes next." Jared led her off into the grass.

They ducked under branches and sidestepped thick bushes. There was a faint outline of a trail, with grass pressed down and spots of dirt visible. She heard a tapping noise and wondered if she'd imagined it, but the sound grew louder with every step they took. Accompanying the sounds, she began to see the dim glow of Psy energy.

"What's that?" she asked.

"You'll see." That twinkle was still in his eye.

He led them farther into the woods and the sounds grew louder. Eventually, they came to a tree-lined arena filled with playing fields of every type, going on for at least a mile. There were areas courted off for basketball, football, volleyball, tennis, baseball, and soccer. To their right was a series of racks filled with balls, bats, rackets, replacement nets, helmets, and anything else you could possibly need to play any sport. And people were everywhere. They jumped, swung, sprinted, and laughed. A group of men played full-contact football, plowing into each other to the ground, then helping each other get back to their feet.

"A sports park? I thought they closed down the last one of these years ago."

Sports weren't illegal, but they were frowned upon. They're competitive, and competition breeds strong emotion, and strong emotions led to Psy violations and injuries. Some people died. The riots from the last World Series spilled over into five counties and lasted for thirteen days. When it was over, there were a thousand dead. Over half had no visible signs of what'd killed them. After that, all major sporting events were canceled.

"Where do they get all the equipment?" She picked up a ball and examined it.

"There's a guy who knows how to do coding for the printers. Give him a description of anything you need and he can get it printed. So what's your sport?"

Even through the inhibitor band, Lexy could feel him busting with excitement. As she looked around, her stomach fluttered, eyes grew wider. She wanted to jump into all of the games. The world was filled with brightness and color she'd never noticed before. People were cheering and smiling. They were active, making their own pleasure, not sitting around waiting for it. They were living.

She stared at the volleyball net. "My parents and I used to play volleyball when I was a kid. Mom was always on my team, with Dad on the other side. Even with the two of us, we still had trouble beating him."

She could still remember the old football jersey her father would wear. It was faded and worn through in spots, but he loved it. And after their games, they would go inside for cookies and popcorn and veg out watching old horror movies. Her father kept his old movie collection and DVD player, even after everyone went digital. He did the same with his books. Her family owned many banned movies and content deleted from the cloud. Wary of the censorship that grew stricter with every year, her father had bought and stored several DVD players and replacement parts. Her mother now kept the last working one at her house. Because Lexy had a roommate, it wasn't safe for her to keep it. She missed watching those old movies.

"Volleyball it is." Jared grabbed her hand back to led her to the court. He grabbed a ball from a small metal rack on the side and tossed it to her. "Your serve."

She tossed up the ball and swung her hand at it. The result was a pathetic arch and the ball hit the net. To top it off, it landed outside the court.

"I forgot how bad I was." She laughed. "Then again, I was like four-feet tall the last time I played."

Jared walked over to where the ball rolled and picked it up. "Maybe I should serve."

"Might be for the best."

He served, and she did her best to return the ball. It took a couple fumbling hits, but she managed to get it back over the net and in the court. After a few more passes, she felt less like a giraffe walking across ice. Ten minutes in, she actually managed to score a point. She jumped and whooped. Then he began to throw her harder and trickier shots. She missed most of them, but landed a few.

"Well," Jared put the volleyball back in the rack, "I think the final score was around fifty-six to three."

Lexy giggled. "Probably, but I don't even care. That was fun."

"I'm glad you had a good time. We can come back whenever you want."

"Thanks."

He held out his arm, and she took it and leaned against him as they strolled along. The football game was still going on, and people had gathered around to watch. There were a few children in the group and many women calling out support for players. Several couples watched and played other games. Some held hands. Kisses were stolen between blocks and passes. People walked off and arrived from many directions.

"How did you find this place?"

"My dad. He knows a lot of people."

"You said you work for him. What do you do? How do you have time for all the things you learn?"

"I help him keep the books straight for his business. He pretty much lets me do it whenever I want, as long as I get it done.

"What kind of business is it?"

Jared inhaled deeply. "He's... part of the entertainment industry."

She snorted. "You make it sound like he's running a brothel."

Jared kept walking and led them to the tree stump where they'd changed shoes.

He retrieved the skates from where he'd left them. "Told you they'd still be here. You want to walk back or skate?"

"Walk. But don't change the subject. What does your dad do?" She took her skates from him.

"He helps people. Everything he does is so he can help people." Sincerity and discomfort was in his eyes.

Lexy went to him and put a hand on his face. "I—"

Jared captured her mouth in a kiss. Her hand dropped and her body went limp in his arms. She barely registered the skates falling to the ground. His lips were firm but gentle. There was power behind his touch, but she felt she could step away at any moment and he would let her go. He touched the side of her face, and his finger brushed over her inhibitor band, snapping her out of the moment. She stepped back and tried to regain her composure. Her eyes flickered to his inhibitor band.

"Is that the first time you've been kissed?" Jared bent over to pick up their skates and then slung both pairs over his shoulder.

She turned sideways and crossed her arms. "No one does that anymore. No one wants to. Everyone just wants to Psy-play."

"Except you?"

Lexy pursed her lips and looked down.

"Well, they don't know what they're missing, cause that was pretty amazing."

She grinned but remained silent.

"Look," he took a step toward her, "I'm not going to lie. I like you. I like spending time with you. I like talking and doing things with you. I think people can be too casual with how they connect. They think if it isn't physical, it isn't real. But Psy contact can be just as real as physical contact. I don't think there's anything wrong with being picky about who you connect with."

Lexy dropped her arms and shuffled closer to him. "I like you, too, just so you know." She gave him a peck on the lips, and her heart was pounding. Her body shook and her breath caught in her throat. "And I like connecting with you."

Jared grinned. "Come on. Since we're walking, there's something else I want to show you."

They ambled off the trail, deep into the forest, in the opposite direction of the sports park. The sun began to dip low in the mid-afternoon sky and much of the light was blocked by the trees.

At last, they came to a small clearing filled with unusually shaped trees. A maze of roots, trunks, and branches formed natural bridges, arches, and alcoves. Feeling a like a kid again, Lexy broke away and darted around one of the trees. She stepped up on a root and climbed to a branch. Jared jumped and grabbed onto the branch and swung up to join her. With another jump, he went higher and reached down to help her up. The view was unlike any she could remember. With leaves at their backs and the ground far below, she felt safe.

"How amazing would it be to have a house right here in this tree," she said.

Jared grinned and stood. "Come this way."

He led her down one of the branches and stepped onto the branch of another tree, on the way to the ground. Darting between the trees, he led her to another clearing, and Lexy's jaw drop. In the middle of an open field, stood a massive tree like the ones they'd just climbed. Only, in this tree, hidden between the branches, was a wood cabin. The roots curved into a ramp leading up to a small set of steps. She followed him up and onto the front porch of the house. The view was as incredible as the last tree they were in. She could see a great distance in every direction from the circular porch that ramped up onto higher branches and a crow's nest room above the house.

"Is this yours?"

"All mine."

"Then why do you have an apartment in town? If this place was mine, I'd never leave here."

Jared chuckled and opened the front door to show her inside. He tapped a couple push lights and lit some candles. The inside was open, with a basic living room, a loft bed near the crow's nest hatch, and a kitchenette complete with a camp stove and a supply of non-perishable foods. They climbed up to the loft and through the hatch. Inside the crow's nest was round pillow big enough for both of them to sit on, and a bookshelf full of old books, most of them now censored in their electronic formats. There was also a door that led out onto the porch ramp. From the nest, she could see a lake. Past that was even more trees. No city lights were visible.

"I stay in town to be closer to my dad. But I come out here as often as I can. No one else lives around here. We're a couple miles from the sports park or anywhere else people go."

"A couple miles? I didn't realize we walked for that long."

He nodded. "It can be easy to lose track of time and distance out here."

She leaned back against him and looked up. Her lips brushed his cheek, and she felt him take a deep breath. She wondered if they kissed again now, would it would go further. Her body ached as she anticipated exploring his body. He held her tight, securely, protectively. She tilted her head up, and he kissed her. She turned her body into his, and he pressed her back into the pillow. His body covered hers. He trailed his hands along her sides and caressed her breasts, over her blouse. She shivered and pressed her pelvis against his. Then his light surged and she felt herself falling, awash in desire. It pulled back almost as soon as it appeared, but she found herself blinking from the after-image of his strong energy. She looked up and expected to see his inhibitor band gone, but he still wore it.

She pushed back and sat up. "I'm sorry." Her voice was breathless and raspy.

"No, you don't have to apologize. I'm sorry. I... I got carried away."

He straightened his clothes and opened the floor hatch to let them down into the main room. After entering the kitchenette, he took out a bottled water from under the counter and handed it to her before pulling out a second one for himself.

"We should start heading back if we want to make it to town before dark," he said.

"You going to the club tonight with Kara and Curtis?"

"Which club?"

"I don't know. She said it was some new one."

"You going?"

"Probably," she rolled her eyes. "Kara doesn't like to take no for an answer. She's determined to get me out, for my own good."

Jared held open the front door for her and followed her out. "Well, send me a text if you get dragged along, and I'll be there. If it gets too bad, we can check out early."

"Sounds like a plan."

They walked in silence most of the way back. Once they reached the path, they put their skates back on to reduce the time it would take to get back to the cars. Even so, it was already dark when they reached the parking lot.

Lexy opened her door and sat down to remove the skates. She stood without putting on the sneakers, and the concrete poked at her toes and sent a chill through her socks.

"I had a great time today," she said.

"Me, too."

He held up a hand and she held up hers to meet it.

Reluctantly, they let go and got into their cars. As Lexy drove away, she stared in her rearview mirror until his car was no longer visible.

4

The Pulse nightclub was an impressive site. Brick, white with blue and purple specks, made up the front and sides of the building. There were no windows, only a series of external arches to provide the illusion of windows. Massive crystal towers sat at the four corners, protecting everyone in the streets from Psy pulses from the patrons. Emblazoned on the front double doors was a circle with a line down the center. On the line was a smaller circle and a series of smaller lines splaying out in several directions. It had the appearance of a spider, though not exactly. The symbol stood for all Psy abilities and indicated a free zone. Within that building, Psy usage was allowed with little restriction.

The walls were soundproof, and every time the doors opened, a blast of music filled the street. Once the doors closed, the only sounds in the streets were from the people waiting to go inside. Lines stretched for two blocks in either direction. People begged and bribed to get in, but the bouncers kept the numbers under control. For every person who came out, another one went in. Since most of the club goers were there for the night, if you didn't get in with the first couple waves, and if you weren't near the front of the line, your chances of entering before dawn were nearly zero. That is unless you knew someone, which Ben did. He waved to the bouncer and called him by name, and he and his group went right in.

Lights and sounds pummeled them the moment the door was opened. Lexy braced herself. The others removed their bands and linked them through a belt loop. Lexy waited at the threshold, afraid to take that final step in, when she felt a hand at her back. Jared smiled back at her, and she found herself moving through the door. She watched him out the corner of her eye, but he didn't remove his band. Relieved not to be the only one wearing a band, she held onto his hand at her waist. His presence was a reassurance. He wasn't judging her.

Finally feeling more at ease, she took in her surroundings. The entrance foyer was dimly lit, a transition from the outside. After walking through a beaded curtain, they entered a black room with white lines next to the ceiling and edging all counters and furniture. There was a black light bar where glasses were lined with fluorescent paint and the bottles on the rack were illuminated from behind by faint-colored lights. In the center of the room, red, blue, and green ceiling lights spun around to shine in every direction. There was an area of tables and booths. The booths were enclosed in scrolled wire half-walls to give them privacy. The lighting was also dimmer in that area. Electric candle lanterns hung on the walls, and each booth had a beaded curtain at its entrance. From behind a few curtains, Lexy could hear moans and see movement in the flickering light. Just outside the booths, young people sat at the tables, drinking and talking.

The highlight of the club was the dance floor. Past an intricate wire banister, down a short set of stairs, people danced through a floor covered in white sudsy foam, glowing from black lights hung overhead. A waterfall of foam fell down between two cages with scantily clad women dancing inside. As they gyrated and moaned, other people used the edge of their platforms to jump out onto the floor, where they were caught and carried into the crowd.

"Let's get drinks first," Curtis said.

The girls took a seat at one of the tables and waited for the men to get their drinks. Lexy took a breath. Even with her band on, the Psy energy was intense. She felt a little like she was moving through syrup. Her eyes were already feeling the strain from the glow around everyone, though it wasn't too bad as long as she didn't look at the dance floor too long. That was the source of the strongest Psy pulses.

"Kara, what's wrong with your roommate?" Ben's girlfriend, Monique, was staring at Lexy. "I mean, what exactly do you have to hide that you won't take your band off in here? We're in a Psy zone, for crying out loud. Or are you too good for the rest of us? Can't stand to mix your energies with us?"

"Monique, that's enough." Kara said. "If she doesn't want to go Psy, what do you care? It's none of your business."

"Maybe because no one wants to party with a Psude," Trae's date said. "She wouldn't take that band off her head if it was on fire."

Lexy looked across the room to the bar, but Jared and the others were still ordering drinks. They wouldn't be back for another couple minutes, at least.

"I'm going to the restroom." She stood.

She didn't notice Monique stand until it was too late. With the help of Trae's date, she disengaged Lexy's band and took it off before she could react. Light was all she could see. Blazing white, blue, and purple light filled her field of vision. Energy vibrated the air around her. What felt like syrup a moment before, now felt like a pulsing swarm of insects. No longer knowing which direction was up or down, she stumbled, only vaguely able to feel her feet. Every person had a unique Psy signature, complete with color patterns. The pattern always flared white when someone pulsed. She could follow that pulse to its target, seeing their light flare in emotional response. The flare was greatest at the moment of psygasm. Even with her eyes closed, she could see the lights. Her body felt weightless. Her mind was swimming. There were too many lights to distinguish between them. Too many pulses blended together.

Then all the lights went out. Feeling nauseous, she opened her eyes hesitantly and saw Jared sitting beside her in a plain, dim room. Multi-facetted crystals lined the wall. This was a crystal room, a private sanctuary for those who needed a rest from Psy, or a rendezvous option for those who wished for more privacy than the booths afforded. The bed underneath her and small private bath suggested this room was intended for couples wishing to engage in syntercourse—a combination of real and Psy sex.

She wondered at Jared's light, no brighter than usual, until she saw the dial by the front door was turned to Full Block. Depending on how the crystals were turned, they either blocked out all Psy impulses in their area, or they simply blocked Psy energy from traveling through them, as the crystals outside the club did.

"How're you feeling?" Jared moved a wet wash rag over her forehead and brushed his thumb over her hand.

"Okay now. Do you have my band?"

"No, I didn't see it when I grabbed you. I'll have to go look for it."

"I'm sorry."

"Why are you sorry!"

"For being so much trouble." She pushed up to a seated position, feeling stronger now with the crystals and Jared.

Embarrassment filled the void left by her panic.

"Don't worry about it. I'll go get your band and we can go. It'll be fine."

Before she could argue, there was a knock at the door. Kara slowly pushed it open and peeked in before entering.

Curtis followed, holding Lexy's inhibitor band. "Thought you could use this." He handed it to her.

Ben came in next and closed the door. "I'm so sorry about that. We went to a club before this and Monique can get a little crazy sometimes when she's riding a Psy-high. She doesn't think about what she's doing, and she can be really selfish."

"That's okay," Lexy said. "No harm done." She put on her band and stood. "In any case, I just want to go home."

"I'll drive you." Jared took her arm and led her through the club, straight outside to his car.

He helped her in, and she sat back for the ride. Her face was reflected in the car window, creating a transparent scene overlay to the hills and cars. There was no moon, only a black field covered in stars. Car lights blinked as people turned onto the autopilot lane onramp. Jared drove past them.

"Where are we going?" she asked.

"Your apartment."

"But we missed the turn."

"I never take the wired roads. At least, not when I have a choice. Been on them a couple times, but I can't stand not being in control of my car."

They drove down service roads and by residential neighborhoods, passing a dozen other onramps filled with cars waiting to be merged into traffic. Lexy looked at the many windows, mostly showing single individuals sitting down to eat or flipping through images on their tablets. Occasionally, she'd see multiple people talking or playing a card game. The biggest missing thing she noticed were families. Nowhere did she see children playing or toys strewn about the rooms.

They pulled up to her apartment building and she looked

up at her darkened window, realizing how similar it would look to anyone driving past. She was no different than everyone else in the city. She may not participate in all the Psy activities, but she didn't have much else to show for her life.

Jared opened her door and helped her out.

"Thanks for the ride."

"No problem." He followed her inside.

She wasn't in the mood to be alone, so she didn't argue. The printer whirled and buzzed. Through the viewing window, she could see Kara's latest purchase printing.

Jared followed her into the kitchen and started rummaging through the cabinets and pantries. "Got anything to snack on? I haven't eaten anything since breakfast."

"There's some toaster pastries and sandwich stuff. I think we still have some peanut butter, if you want that on some bread."

"Sounds good."

"She pulled out the bread and got to work. When she handed the plate to Jared, he looked up at her and grinned.

"You drew a star on it?"

She looked at the open-faced sandwich with a star drawn into the peanut butter, and shrugged. "Habit, I guess. That's how my mom always does it."

Still grinning, he sat on the sofa and started eating. He thanked her when she brought him a glass of water.

He put down the empty plate and sat back. "So how are you feeling?"

"I'm fine."

"I've never seen anyone react like that to removing their band, and I've been around quite a few people their first time unchained."

"I don't really want to talk about it. You know, like how you didn't want to talk about your father's work?"

"Fair enough. I'll let it drop for now."

"I appreciate you bringing me home, but you don't have to stick around."

"Do you think I care that you can't go Psy?"

She gulped. "Most people would."

"Most people are idiots."

She couldn't help laughing at his bluntness.

"There are plenty of things you can do without Psy."

Lexy thought back to the tree house and felt her cheeks flush. She still wondered at the flare of light she saw, but there was no way to ask about it without telling him what she could see.

After taking his plate, she went back into the kitchen to give herself time to think. That moment was short. Jared reached around her to put his glass in the sink. Pressed his chest against her back, resting his other hand on her shoulder. She leaned into him and turned her head to rub her cheek against his chin. He groaned and turned her around to face him. They kissed, and her body shivered. She wanted his touch, his real touch. How did people live without this? Her body was on fire for him. She didn't want to be one of the empty people behind the window anymore. She felt an energy around him and opened her eyes. His eyes had a strange blue glow around them. His touch left trails of light across her skin.

"Which way is your room?" he asked.

"This one." She pointed.

They moved that way. After entering, they both reached out to close the door. Her hands and lips were focused on him. Somehow, they made it to her bed without tripping over her skates. Then he was on top of her. The rough edge of his stubble rubbed against her face. He pulled her shirt from her pants, and she did the same. He pulled her buttons loose and let her shirt fall open, revealing the curve of her breasts, covered by a light blue lace bra. He kissed her chest, nibbling at the skin above her bra. She arched her back. Clumsily, she began pulling her pants down. Each tug put her lower regions in contact with his. She wiggled them all the way off and kicked the bunched-up denim onto the floor.

Jared's shirt followed. She splayed her hands against his skin and leaned forward, twisting around to kiss his bare chest. Her tongue flicked across his nipple and she trailed wet kisses down his side, sucking on the skin until he moaned and undid his pants. With one hand working on his pants, he used the other to work on her. Slipping his fingers into her hidden moistness, he touched her softly at first, exploring her folds. He continued rubbing her outside with his thumb while using his fingers to delve deep inside. He kissed her mouth again and finished removing his pants. Then after pulling off her under-garment, he pushed inside in two easy strokes.

Lexy saw stars. She felt weightless. In her arms, Jared was the only thing real in the world. He moved in her, and soon she was moving, too. Sweating, moaning, and clinging to each other, they fell into the maelstrom of their shared experience. They shook as their energy left them. Jared collapsed beside her, pulling her into his arms. She let her breathing slow and ran her fingers over his chest. Eyes closed, she listened his heartbeat.

Then she realized, they hadn't used protection. Physical sex was so rare, it was difficult to find contraceptives. It wasn't cost-effective for stores to carry them. Sexually transmitted diseases were uncommon enough for no one to worry about that, and most people who had real sex wanted to get pregnant. The irony was that, while fewer people were opting to have chil-dren, women were more fertile than they had been in a century. Once they stopped taking synthetic birth control, many of the fertility problems and other health issues of the past several decades cleared up. That realization led to further hormone research and a shift to herbal remedies to correct imbalances that did occur. Women were now more likely to get pregnant and better able to maintain healthy pregnancies.

"That was some risk you took," she whispered.

"The best things in life are."

She agreed. Jared was a risk she wanted to take.

5

Kara and Curtis were both home when Lexy awoke the next morning. Jared left some time during the night after his father called needing help with something. Unable to go back to sleep, Lexy got up for a quick shower and changed her clothes. She was just finishing loading the sheets into the washing machine, when Kara and Curtis emerged from Kara's room. Thankfully, they took her comments from the previous day to heart and limited their Psyplay in the living room.

"Good morning," Lexy said.

"Good morning," Kara crooned. "So I noticed Jared's car was still here when we got in last night."

"Mmm-hmmm." Lexy hid a grin behind her cup.

"Don't *mmm-hmmm* me. I want details."

"I doubt you'll get anything out of her." Curtis took a seat at the counter. "If I know Jared, he was a perfect gentleman last night."

"Yeah, right," Kara scoffed. "That's why you're doing laundry so early in the morning. And don't try to tell me it's just work clothes, because I saw you put your blue bed sheets in there."

"You don't ever wash your sheets?" Lexy said. "Because that's gross."

Kara grunted. "You are so frustrating. You know that, right?"

Curtis laughed and patted Kara on the back. "Why don't you go get changed so we can go? If we hurry, we can make it to the restaurant while they're still serving breakfast."

After a few seconds, Kara disappeared into her room.

"Thanks," Lexy said.

She was starting to warm up to Curtis. Then again, he was friends with Jared, so he couldn't be too bad.

"No problem. I'm sorry about what happened last night. You really don't have any tolerance for Psy, do you?"

She nodded and shrugged.

"Well, it seems you and Jared are really hitting it off."

She nodded again, smiling at the mention of his name.

Curtis looked back to make sure they were still alone. Then he turned back to her. "Honestly, I've never seen him this happy before. I'm probably stepping over the line, but I think you should know, he's a Forcer."

Lexy's heart skipped.

Psy-forcers were strong Psy users, capable of inflicting their touch on those wearing an inhibitor band. No one was safe from them and everyone feared them, so they usually hid their identities until an errant thought revealed them. No one could hide for long without an extreme level of self-control and willpower.

She thought back to all the flares of light she'd seen from him, and it made sense. Even so, those flares were brief, and with all the intimate contact they had, he never overtly pulsed at her. Everything from the previous night had been physical. How much control must it have taken to hold back his Psy energy while doing what they did?

Lexy opened her mouth to ask a question, but the bedroom door opened and Kara came out.

"All right, I'm ready. Let's go." She strode to the door and picked up her purse and keys from the small table there.

Curtis jumped down from his seat. "Coming." Then he leaned back toward Lexy and whispered, "He's a good guy. Just thought you should know."

* * *

"LAST ONE IS OUT." Jared dusted off his hands and took a seat at the bar.

Mick slid a drink down to him and continued cleaning the bar. He wore a red bow tie and suspenders over his white shirt. Always trying to recreate some look from the past. It was part of his charm. You never knew which era he would dress in. One night, he may come dressed as a southern gentleman. Another night, he was wearing a top hat and tails. But this look was his favorite. Jared always joked that he was born in the wrong century. Mick argued that they all were.

He put down his washcloth and closed the liquor cabinet. "It was a good thing you could come in last night. After Brian left, things got a little harry."

Brian was their best bouncer. He was the strongest Shield, able to block Psy ability from those who were out of control. That was useful when dealing with drunk people riding a Psy-high. Jared wasn't a Shield, but he could always use his Forcer strength to get people in line.

"What happened to Brian, anyway? Dad was in such a rush last night, he never said."

Mick grinned from ear to ear. "His wife went into labor, so he had to get back to their house in the free zone. He just texted about ten minutes ago, while you were seeing that one guy to the cab. It's a girl."

Jared beamed. "Now that's good news. Makes what now? Five?"

"Six. Three boys and three girls, all spitting images of their mom, thank goodness."

They chuckled.

Jared finished his drink. "I'm going to have to get out there for a visit someday soon. Things have just gotten kind of busy."

"Yeah? Where've you been the past couple nights?"

"Different places."

He started stacking the chairs up on the tables, while Mick took out the mop and began cleaning the floors.

"I met a girl," Jared said.

"Oh, yeah? You going to bring her around here so we can give our approval?"

"Not yet. She's a little skittish around Psy energy. Nearly passed out when someone took her band off down at that new club last night."

"Hmm. Seen a few of those back in the early days, but haven't seen anyone like that in a while. Then again, people like that don't usually frequent these joints."

"I took her to the park and the treehouse."

Mick stopped mopping and looked up. "You must be pretty serious about this girl."

"We just met, but I can't explain the way I feel when I'm around her. She's got a good heart and tries to help people around her, even if they're strangers. When we're together, it just feels right."

"You've got it bad." He went back to mopping.

Jingling bells signaled the front door opening.

Jared looked up and his mouth dropped open. "Lexy?"

She looked over at him and smiled nervously. "Hi, umm, can we talk?"

He looked over at Mick, who was grinning again.

"Go. I've got the rest."

Jared went to Lexy and led her back outside. His apartment was only a couple buildings down from the club. It would give them the most privacy to talk.

"How did you find me?"

"I went to your apartment first. When you weren't there, I looked around and I... just had a feeling you were here."

"Okay. Well," he opened his door and turned on the light, "welcome to my home. It's not much, but it's a place to sleep."

Not much was generous. His apartment was an efficiency with just enough room to fit a twin-sized bed and a nightstand.

"Can I get you something to drink?"

"I know you're a Psy-forcer."

His smile vanished. He drifted over to her and put a hand up, inches from her face. "I would never touch you against your will. Psychically or otherwise."

Lexy could see the sincerity and fear in his eyes. She was grateful for the headband, because in that moment all she could think about was touching him.

"How do you control it? I thought all Forcers lived in isolation, from fear of exposure."

He lowered his hand and took a step back, relief flashing across his face. "My father is a Forcer. Since it runs in families, he taught me control techniques, from the time I was born, long before my abilities manifested. I can even control it when I'm asleep. The only time I have any trouble with it is when I'm sick or medicated, but that's why I have the treehouse. I go there when that happens and hold out until I feel better."

"Then how did Curtis know?"

He gave a wry grin. "So that's how you found out. Well, my former best friend was with me once, when I got food poisoning. He got me to the treehouse and called my family's doctor.

"What's your range?"

His posture relaxed. "Thirty feet, with bands. Without, I'm not sure. I've gone as far as fifty feet, with one person wearing a band. Doesn't seem to matter much if I'm the one wearing it or the other way around. Both without bands, I know I can go farther, but I've never been able to test the limits. Of course, the contact precision goes down as distance is increased."

Lexy stared at him, eyes wide, mouth gaping. He was taking a great risk by telling her any of this, yet he answered all her questions without hesitation.

"There's a reason I never take off my band, why I reacted like I did at the club, and why I knew where you were." Her chest tightened from the fear. "I'm a Psy-reader."

His gaze flicked to hers.

"I also inherited it from my father. Unfortunately, he didn't learn the same control techniques your father did. He didn't have to."

"A police officer?"

She nodded.

At one time, Psy-readers were respected, sought out. In a world where thoughts could kill without leaving any evidence, Readers could look at a person and see into their hearts.

"He was a detective before the Storm. In the aftermath he used his ability, to track Psy killers and other Psy criminals. Then the bands were invented and the focus turned from investigations to purging, and anyone with a strong ability was targeted. Readers became as feared as everyone else. My father, and those like him, became a liability. Their families and careers were threatened until they turned on each other. My father kept his head low for a while and prepared for me and my mother to get to safety. But they eventually caught up with him, and he was charged with Conspiracy to Commit Thought Crime and sentenced to an undefined term in prison." She laughed, hysterically. "They say Psy-crime went down after the bands, but it's all a lie. The government just brokered a deal where the media stopped reporting it. The theory was, the less people heard about crime, the less they would think about it.

As the reported crimes went down, people thought it was true, but the real numbers never changed. The police knew the truth, but they were all issued court orders to prevent them from discussing it. Anyone who discovered the truth or even wrote about fictional crime was arrested for disturbing the peace. Those crimes weren't reported either. My father helped the ones he could, before his arrest. I haven't seen him in over fifteen years, and my mother and I have been in hiding ever since."

"How strong is your reading?"

"I get impressions and can tell if someone is lying, even if they have on the band. When the band is off, I see these bright lights inside and around everyone. Even if I'm not looking at them or they're in another room, I can see their light. It's like a fingerprint. Everyone's light is different. It moves differently. If they're pulsing, I can see it and who it's directed to. Sometimes I hear thoughts riding the pulse waves. After a certain distance, the lights blend together and the edges of my vision become whitewashed. When I came here and you weren't home, I felt and saw your energy down the street and followed it."

"Okay, two things. You sensed me from here, with your band on?"

She nodded.

"That's gotta be at least a hundred feet."

She shrugged.

"What's your range?"

"I don't know. When the lights blend together, I can't tell how far away they are."

"Second question. You hear thoughts? I didn't think anyone could do that."

"There aren't many who can. My father only knew of one."

"I can see why your father did what he did. If they found out what you can do—"

"There wouldn't be a trial. They'd kill me on the spot or find a way to use me. I know."

"You took a great risk telling me all this."

"So did you."

They were quiet for several heartbeats.

"I could teach you the techniques I use," Jared said. "It could help you control your ability. The more control you have over it, the more likely you are to notice threats. It could save your life."

"I don't know." Lexy took a few steps back and crossed her arms, trying to rub away the goosebumps. "I'm not taking the band off, and I can hardly sense anything through it."

He narrowed his eyes. "I'm not entirely convinced of that, especially if you sensed me all the way from here, with your band on. But all the same, that's why you could wear one of these." He pulled off his headband and handed it to her. "It looks and feels like a regular band, but the inhibitor chip is disabled. It's done to look like a defect, so if anyone ever decides to check it—which never happens unless you get arrested—you can always claim you didn't know, that your Psy ability was too weak to notice. They let you off with a warning and you thank them profusely for discovering the defect."

She handed the band back to him. "I don't think I want to feel everything all the time. The band isn't so bad. It's quiet."

"Once I help you, it can be like that without the band. You can select what to let in and keep out." He pointed to her chest. "You choose," and then her head, "not the band. Don't you want to learn what it's like to be who you really are, undiluted?" He grabbed her hands. "I know you're afraid. There's nothing wrong with that. But I'm here and I'll help you every step of the way."

"You barely know me."

"I'd say I know you fairly well."

She pulled her hands from his and took a step back. "I'm sorry. I can't."

"Do you trust me?"

Her eyes watered, breath caught in her chest. "I... I do."

"Then come with me. Let me show you what life could be like. Then if you still want to wear the band, I won't try to stop you. I won't ask again."

"Where are we going?"

"To the treehouse."

6

Jared drove, off the wired roads as he had the night before. They went toward the skating park but passed it and turned off on a barely used service road that swept around the park. He followed the road for so long that Lexy began to feel hypnotized by the many shadows in front of them. Large trees, much like the ones near his sanctuary, lined their path. Eventually, he turned onto a small dirt road that Lexy would've missed had she been driving. Dirt turned to gravel and then to grass. After a few minutes, they were no longer on anything resembling a road. He stopped beside a small lake with a dock and wooden fishing poles sticking up out of the ground. After taking off his inhibitor band and putting it on the dash of the car, he got out.

"Where's the house?"

"Past that line of trees." He pointed. All this is on my land. Care for a swim?"

"I didn't bring a suit."

He grinned, mischievously. "We're the only ones here, and I have electric sensors around the edge of the property line. If anyone crosses it, an alert gets sent to my watch." He pulled off his shirt and pants and jumped into the water with just his boxer shorts on. "Come on in."

Lexy took off her shirt and shorts, folded them and put them on the ground, by his clothes. Even after the previous night, she still felt self-conscious standing in front of him in her underwear.

"You can take your band off, too."

Lexy stiffened. "I told you, I'm not going Psy."

"There's no one around for miles."

"You're here."

"I can block my mind as well as the strongest inhibitor band. You won't sense anything from me unless you want to, but the choice is yours." He flipped onto his back and started swimming out into the lake.

Lexy watched him for a minute. She touched her band and put her hands down twice before she grabbed the band and clicked the disengage buttons. Braced for a shock, she was surprised when she felt nothing more than the same hum of his Psy energy she felt before. The haze of energy around him was a little brighter, but otherwise, he was holding it back as he promised.

She put the band on the ground and moved away from it, every step like something from her dreams. By the time she made it to the end of the dock, she was running. She leaped and dove into the lake, then took off with an underwater sprint and broke the surface a good distance into the lake. While treading water, she reached up for the band and felt only hair and head. Tears rolled down her face. She felt free for the first time in her life.

Jared swam by her and she followed. They splashed and played. She laughed and smiled so hard her cheeks hurt. And then he pulled her to him and they kissed. She saw his light flare for a split second, and then it was down again.

He groaned. "You do make it hard."

"I should hope so," she said.

"Oh, really?" He pulled her with him, out of the water and kissed her on the bank. "Would you care to check?"

"I don't think that's necessary. You're shorts don't leave much to the imagination."

"Then perhaps I should remove them, since they aren't fulfilling their intended function."

"Your logic is sound."

He chuckled. "Well, if we're using logic, these have got to go, too." He leaned down and bit her breast through her transparent bra.

She reached back and unhooked it.

He tossed it beside their other clothes. "That's more like it." He buried his head in her chest, licking and sucking the wet skin.

"Aren't you forgetting something?"

"Hmmm? Oh, yeah."

He reached down and pulled off his boxers, while she removed her panties. Then he slid down her body and buried his face in her. She moaned and clutched at the grass, pulling several pieces from the ground. While licking her, he reached around and slipped a finger inside, driving her mad with the different sensations. She felt her wetness again and urged him up with her hips. He rose and stretched out on top of her, preparing to enter her. But Lexy surprised him by pushing him over onto the ground. After taking her place on top, she speared onto his rigid manhood and arched her back. He moved his hands to her breasts and she rode him slowly. Then, as her feelings grew stronger, she flattened her body over his and kissed him hard, their hands intertwined over their heads. His body rocked as he spilled his seed into her. Her climax came shortly after.

After taking several minutes to rest, they jumped back into the lake to wash off and then walked naked, clothes in hand, to his treehouse. Jared pulled out some towels from the small bathroom and tossed one to Lexy. They dried off and climbed into the loft bed, leaving their clothes on the floor. Jared put his arm around her shoulder and held her close, playing with her breasts as they stared out through the small window by his bed.

"It's nice not to have to hide, for once," Lexy said. "Having any kind of relationship has been impossible. Sooner or later, they all want you to go band-less. Even my friends don't understand. They can't understand. Honestly, Kara's the only friend I have."

"I can't say I know exactly what you've been through. My father is a powerful man. He inspires loyalty. Even though I had to learn to hide what I could do, I've always been around people who knew who I was. Curtis was the only one outside that circle who I ever confided to, and that was out of necessity."

"I hope you're not too mad at him for telling me."

"No. After the concert, he saw the way I watched your car as you drove away. He said something to me. I can't even remember what it was now. I told him I was bringing you here. He knew what that meant. I don't bring anyone here."

Lexy snuggled in closer and felt his arms tighten around her.

"Can you see anything now?" he asked.

"Yes."

"What do you see?"

She pushed away just enough to look at him. "A humming glow—white, with streaks of turquoise and midnight blue. It's everywhere around you." She reached up and gestured. "When you flare, I see a white light brighten at your chest." She touched his heart. "And sometimes I see a light flash from your eyes."

"You see this all the time?"

She nodded. "What do you see when you look at people?"

"Nothing. I just see the person. Does everyone look like that?"

"There are different colors, usually greens or purples. Pulses are usually just white, though I've seen a few with ribbons of color snaking through. It depends on how strong the thought is, on how much of themselves they're putting into the contact."

"You said you see a humming glow. What do you mean by humming?"

"I see it, but I also feel and hear it. When I close my eyes, the vibrations form a picture in my mind. I see flashes of lights and colors swirling over darkness. Sometimes they show the outlines of people. Other times, it's just light."

"All that sounds beautiful."

"I guess I've never really thought of it like that. When there's a lot of Psy energy and pulsing, it feels like I'm being pummeled by continuous waves, and it becomes a suffocating pressure. When someone pulses, I can see where it comes from and who they touch. So instead of a bunch of individual lights, I see light everywhere."

She hadn't realized how animated she was until she felt his hand on her arm. His light warmed her skin, sending calming emotions to her.

"You're doing it now without even realizing it." She looked back up at him.

He furrowed his brow.

"Your hand is glowing."

The glow went out. All his light dimmed as he clamped down on his energy, and her arm grew cold again.

"It's okay," she said. "Everyone does it. Our Psy energy follows our thoughts and desires. When you want to comfort someone, some of your energy goes into that. Even inhibitor bands and crystals don't block out all the transfer. People just don't realize it. It's not enough for anyone to notice, unless you can see it."

She put her hand back on his chest and fed her energy into her palm. His chest filled and his face relaxed.

"That kind of transfer is the only kind I can do."

"You can't pulse?"

She shook her head. "Not very well. I can't focus. I get too distracted by the energy I see and feel from others. The only time I can concentrate is when I have my band on. But that's normal for a Reader. My father told my mom there were only a few police he knew who were as good at reading as pulsing. Usually, we can only pulse with people we're extremely connected to, like a spouse or close friend, or when we're highly emotional or provoked."

He wrapped his fingers around her hand on his chest and the glow returned. Warmth spread through her and her fears melted away.

"Can you show me what it feels like?" she asked.

With one hand holding hers and the other on her back, she felt his soft touch on her face. A hazy trail of light reached out from his constant aura glow. She closed her eyes and saw his ribbons of color all around her. Gentle touches peppered her skin. They started out barely noticeable and grew stronger. She could've sworn she felt his fingers on her. She opened her eyes. The air was full of smoke-like tendrils of light. They encircled her breasts and she felt his lips there. At the same instant, she felt his mouth rain kisses down her side and lower back. All the while, he didn't move. Psychic hands swept down her sides and cupped her bottom. One finger slipped through her legs and inside her. She sucked in a breath. Not restricted by physical limitations, his psychic fingers delved everywhere. His physical hands held her firm, as her body convulsed from pleasure. His phantom fingers slowed and sped up to draw out the experience as long as possible. Just when she thought she couldn't take it anymore, he would back off and bring her to the crest again.

Then Jared did something unexpected. He kissed her, really kissed her. She felt his lips on hers, while his psychic lips remained in other areas. His real tongue plunged into her mouth, as his phantom tongue plunged into other depths. Another mouth sucked on her neck, while still another set of phantom lips remained on her breasts. His knee nudged her legs apart and he pushed into her. She could feel him enter a moment before he actually did. She could still feel his psychic touch licking and touching her sensitive areas outside and in. A wall of ghost hands held her back, pulling her closer to him. She shook and felt her vision fill with flashes of light that had nothing to do with Psy energy. Jared followed and she felt all his psychic hands disappear in a flash of white light, as he lost all focus and control. His energy blinded her, filling the room for an instant, before he could pull it back in. Lexy continued to flutter in his arms.

"So that was syntercourse." Her voice was raspy and dry. She licked her lips and continued to cling to him.

"Yeah." He was out of breath as well. He tightened his grip and buried his head in the crook of her neck. "You okay."

"I'm fantastic."

Jared laughed. "Well, we can do that any time you want."

"I don't know about that. You flared pretty far at the end there. I don't think we could do this anywhere but here, even if you did teach me to control what I sense."

"Hey, give me a break. I think I did pretty good, considering."

"Oh," she giggled, "you did way better than good."

He laughed. "Okay, so let's just live here." He nibbled her neck.

She closed her eyes. "Ohhh, don't tempt me. What about our lives, our work? We can't just drop away from the world."

"Why not?" He moved to her collar bone

She moaned. "Having a hard time coming up with any other arguments right now."

"Good." He sat up and smiled. "Then it's time to go."

"Go? Wait, what? Go where?"

He took her hand and helped her down from the loft bed. He went to their clothes and picked up his shorts, still dripping with lake water.

"Hmm, looks like we'll have to go commando. Unless you want to wear wet underwear." He held up her bra and looked at her, wriggling his eyebrows.

"Actually, that could work either way. Your choice." She raised an eyebrow, then picked up her shirt and pulled it on, sans bra.

He nodded. "Yep, works either way."

Lexy shook her head and pulled on her pants. "Where are we going?"

"To a place where people live without bands."

"No place like that exists."

"They do. And there are more of them than you'd ever know. I'm talking about communities with families and futures, living the way our grandparents did. People marry, have children, and work, all without the bands. They learned to control their Psy energy, like I did."

"What about the government?"

"These cities are hidden in the free zones. The government has no jurisdiction there."

Lexy eyes teared up. A place without the ever-present control of the government. It was too good a dream to hope for. But to live without the band...

She touched her head. Jared handed off her inhibitor band. She held it for several seconds before reluctantly putting it on. She wanted to leave it off, as Jared promised her she could learn to do. But if they were going to a place with un-banded people, she couldn't take the chance of going there unprotected, no matter how much control they may have.

She looked up at him. He squeezed her hand and smiled at her. She felt the slight warmth of his palm. His light was dimmer now. They returned to the car and drove back out to the service road, but they were only on it for a few minutes, when he turned off onto another dirt road.

"We could walk it," Jared said, "but it would take an hour or so, depending on how fast we move. To drive there, we have to go a little out of the way, but it's quicker."

The car bounced over the rocky road. Trees reached over the trail and looked like a green and brown tunnel. Flickers of sunlight danced across their windshield. Lexy's eyes drifted closed. Just before she was about to fall asleep, she felt Jared touch her right cheek. She grinned and watched the tendril of Psy energy get pulled back into him.

"Rest," his voice said, in her mind. "I'll wake you when we're there."

She took a deep breath and let herself fall into sleep.

7

J ared woke her with a kiss. It only took Lexy a moment to sense that something was off. His lips weren't physically touching hers.

She touched her lips and opened her eyes. Looked over at him. "I think you're enjoying that a little too much."

He laughed and leaned over to kiss her for real. "What can I say?" He grinned. "I like being the only one who can touch you. I'm just grateful I can do it without overwhelming you."

"Me, too."

"Come on." He opened the door and walked around to her side to help her out. "I still have so much to show you."

They stood on the cliff of a mountain range. A rusted metal bar rail marked what was once a lookout spot, before people stopped traveling the country with family and friends. Now it was an abandoned relic of a time not that long ago. Below them, deep in the valley, were trees from mountain to mountain.

He led Lexy to the rail and pointed out into the valley. "What do you see?"

"Trees." She looked at him, eyebrows raised.

"Follow me." Still holding on to her arm, he strode to the end of the rail and pushed back an overgrown bush to reveal a set of steps carved into the side of the rock.

She gasped.

The steps were narrow, with no railing for safety. He crept to the steps and helped her head down.

"There are people down there," she said, once they were halfway down the first flight.

Jared looked out. The trees were still all that were visible. It would be another flight before she could see anything else.

"You see their Psy energy from here? Even with your band on?"

She nodded. "Yes, but it's faint. I see flickers of light below the trees." She took a breath. "And now I feel the hum. There are a lot of them."

She could also see the distant shapes of some of the taller buildings. Another flight and they'd be at the bottom.

In a sudden moment of revelation, the village became visible.

"Wow!"

Jared smiled. The many structures reflected the styles of their builders. Some were simple wood cabins. Thatched roof cottages and brick homes rested next to gothic-style buildings and an ornate church at the center of the community. There were a few stand-alone businesses, but most were run out of service sheds attached to homes. The streets were as varied as the buildings. While dirt and grass paths were the norm, there were also cobblestone pathways and a few concrete sidewalks. Children and adults played in the grass or rode bikes on the sidewalks. Vendors sold wares around a massive water fountain near the church. The smell of rich foods drifted from cook houses and backyard barbeques. Some people wore the more reserved clothing of centuries past—hand-sewn dresses, plain white shirts, and slacks. Other people wore synthetic clothing from the time just before the Storm. Still, others wore more modern clothing styles. And everything was hidden under the safety of the mountains and trees.

Lexy took her last few steps without looking down, so engrossed on the people and the buildings. "It's like someone took every century of our history and put them all together."

The church bells rang and everywhere, people put down their games, put up their wares, and hurried to its stained-glass doors.

"Where are they going?"

"It's midday on Sunday. They're going to church."

"Everyone goes?"

"Not everyone, but a good bit do." Jared helped her up onto a set of steps leading up to a series of homes, bridges, ramps, stairs, and sliding poles in the trees. "Back during the early days, before the bands, when families were falling apart and crime was going crazy, a group of priests, ministers, monks, rabbis, shaman, and other holy men got together to discuss what could be done to turn society around. The monks, both native and eastern, shared their meditation and prayer methods for achieving balance and self-control. Through the churches, they offered a refuge for families looking for help. The trees give them cover from satellite and plane sweeps. As far as the outside world is concerned, this place doesn't exist."

"How do they get supplies and medicine here?"

"They are self-sufficient. They grow their own food, raise their own cattle in nearby valleys, and they use herbal remedies. When people are sick, Shield doctors and nurses care for them to prevent accidental Psy incidents."

Shields were people who radiated nullification fields to block Psy ability in their presence. They couldn't pulse and no one could touch them with Psy energy.

"Why don't you do that?" she asked. "Why have your cabin treehouse so far from here?"

"Even a strong Shield can't block me completely."

Her eyes widened.

"I still can't actually touch a Shield. No one can, as far as I know. But I can pulse through their field and touch others."

"I didn't know anyone was that strong."

"Lucky me. Anyway, there are a few doctors who live here and others who travel back and forth, bringing medicine, antibiotics, and other life-saving drugs. Most everything else is cycled through the churches and a few other businesses. That's what my father does. He handles a lot of the logistics. He knows a lot of people, and just about everyone owes him something. He chose to remain in the city, where he could be a greater help.

"So The Den—"

"Is my father's club."

It was one of the oldest Psy dens in the city. It had an *anything goes* reputation and was pretty well left alone. Early in the night, the light clubbers and people just looking for a quick thrill would stop by. From midnight to dawn, the attitude of the club changed. It became full of Psy addicts and the worst of the morally depraved. After midnight, it wasn't safe for anyone of a delicate disposition. Short of murder, you could do nearly anything to anyone without repercussion. And unlike the newer clubs, bands weren't allowed for anyone but the staff. It added to their reputation and gave them some protection from the police. No police officer wanted to come in band-less in a bar full of people who were drunk, Psy-high, and likely to mind rape you the moment you walked through the door.

"Everyone assumes people who live in the free zones are a bunch of Psy addicts just wanting to experience pleasure. There is a fair amount of that on the outside edges, but there's a substantial population of people who just want to live free of the bands. There are artists, musicians, craftsmen, families who shroud themselves in the filth to avoid the scrutiny of the outside world. They just want to live their lives and be left alone."

Jared stopped in front of a wooden door and knocked softly. He heard a wooden chair being pushed back against the floor and then footsteps coming toward them. The door opened a crack at first. Then it was pushed open all the way.

"Jared, what are you doing here?" Brian beamed and motioned for them to enter.

He was a full head taller and much wider than Jared. At the club he looked like a brute, and he had strength to back up his appearance. But at the moment, he looked like a gigantic teddy bear.

"Who's this?"

"Brian, this is Lexy. Lexy, Brian. He works with my father. And Lexy, well, Lexy and I, we..."

"We've been inextricably brought together through the benevolent hand of fate, but otherwise don't know what the heck we're doing." She linked her arm through his and leaned into him.

"Sure, I can go with that," Jared said.

Brian laughed. "Well, all right then. Welcome."

"Uncle Jared!" Brian's two youngest boys, both under hip height ran toward him.

Jared bent down and gave them a hug. "Hey, where's your brother?"

"He's with Mom and the baby," the taller of the two boys answered.

"How are they doing?" Jared asked Brian.

"Good. The baby's doing great. She's sleeping good so far, and she took to nursing right away. They're both asleep right now. The kids and I were just trying to clean up a little so things wouldn't be such a mess when they wake up."

"In that case, we'll get out of your way. I just wanted to say my congratulations."

"Where are you off to?" Brian held the door open and stepped out onto the porch with them.

"The crystal room. I was hoping the teachers there could help Lexy with her Psy control."

"I don't see why they couldn't. They help everyone, even you." He punched Jared in the shoulder.

Lexy looked at them and then down at her feet. "I'm not sure anyone can help me."

"Why's that?" Brian knit his brows and studied her.

Jared looked at Lexy and she nodded.

"She's a Reader. A strong one. She's reading now, even with that band on."

"You don't say. What do you see?"

Lexy took a breath and closed her eyes. With the band on, the humming was faint enough not to bother her, but she could still see the faint glow of Psy energy for every person in Tthe Valley.

"Thirty-one lights on this row of houses. Most of the lights in the homes are children. There are a couple dozen adults in the buildings on the outside edge." She pointed. "Five over there and two there. There are a few others spread around. The church is too bright for me to count how many people are inside." She opened her eyes and looked over at the church. "Their lights blend together. I've never seen so many colors in one place. Usually the light overwhelms them, especially from this distance. But there are colors swirling throughout the entire congregation."

A swirl of light surrounded the church and shot up to the sky. A glow of energy surrounded The Valley, leaving a sparkle in the air. A tear came to her eye and fell down her cheek. The sound of singing came from the church. She closed her eyes again and let herself be bathed in the light and warmth of their Psy energy.

"Daddy, Mom's awake," a little boy called from the door.

"Okay." Brian's voice quivered. "Tell her I'll be right there."

Lexy opened her eyes and turned back to them.

"You two be safe, and good luck."

"Thank you," she said.

Then she and Jared were walking again.

"Are you okay?" he asked.

She nodded.

"I didn't realize you could feel that far with the band on."

"Normally, I can't. At least, not in that detail. This place is charged with energy, in a good way."

It was enough to make her want to take the band off, though she knew it wasn't possible. Still, she wondered what that church service would've felt like without it."

"You said you saw light for the children, but they don't have any Psy ability."

"Everyone has Psy energy inside of them, whether or not they can use it. Even Shields produce a faint glow. Do you really think these teachers can help me?"

He took her hands and pulled her to a stop. "If they can't, then we'll figure it out on our own. There's always a way."

He led her to a beautiful beige and gold building with translucent windows. Difficult to see through, they reflected sunlight in an array of colors. Jared and Lexy stepped through the doors, and she felt the lights outside blink out. Many new Psy signatures inside the building were now visible to her, but they were muted. The inside of the building was full of pillows, incense, and moving water. They stood on a platform that started off narrow and bowled out into a half-circle. To the left was a coy pond. To the right was a sand garden. Glass doors opened out into large sunrooms. Steps on either side of the front door went up to a second floor. In the various rooms, men in robes sat in meditation poses or practiced fighting stances to focus their movements and thoughts. People tended small gardens. Others did intricate wood-working.

"Everyone's different," Jared said. "We all respond to different relaxation techniques, so they have a little bit of everything in here."

"Jared is correct." A young man in an orange and red tunic walked up and offered his hand. "You may remove your band here. The lower level is completely crystaled, for beginners. As you rise through the building, the crystal protection is reduced."

Lexy took off her band and sighed. After years of wearing the inhibitor band, this taste of freedom had taken hold of her heart. She couldn't wait to be through with it, once and for all. There was no way she could go back to the life she had.

She looked around the room and took in the faint lights of Psy energy that signified each person in the building. She could feel their hum now, too. The people in the upper levels were the brightest and strongest, except for Jared. His light was always the easiest for her to read.

"I'm not like the other sixty people in this building," she said.

The young man's eyes widened. "A Reader. And a strong one, too."

"Have you worked with Readers before?" Jared asked.

"A few. I knew some in the early days, but they all disappeared around—"

"Fifteen years ago," Lexy said.

"Yes." He nodded. "I'm Paul."

"Lexy." She took his hand and smiled.

He had a good, honest energy. She remembered her father telling her that he could discern if a person lied just by the hum of his glow. She'd never cultivated her gifts as he had, but she could usually get a sense of a person by his glow. The lights here were loving ones. She felt safe in this place.

"Can you help her?" Jared asked.

"I'd say she's already doing the hard part herself. I've seen that look in many eyes. You've never accepted your gift before now, have you?"

Lexy darted her gaze back at Paul, realizing she'd been analyzing the Psy energy of people in the building. Even now, she felt her eyes trailing back to them, anxious to examine them further. It was like a switch had been turned on. She felt alive. She wanted to read and see all she could.

"I've never been able to focus through the light," she said.

Paul led them down the platform, to a circular hall and brought them into an open courtyard. "From what I remember, that's a common problem for those with your ability. Come this way." He opened a set of patio doors and stepped outside.

She hesitated, but he held out his hand for her to follow. Expecting the worst, she stepped outside and felt stronger sensations than before. She could still see all the individual Psy signatures in the community, except for the group gathered in the church. They were still blurred together. There was the addition of the humming, but she didn't feel waves of pressure rolling against her.

"The lights here are different, aren't they?" Paul said.

She nodded.

"That's because we teach control and not fear. Because of the bands, people in the city never learn to control their ability. They only know how to react. And just like a drowning man, they'll pull you under if you get too close. Here, no one's drowning."

He led her back inside and lit a candelabra set on a table surrounded by mats. Each of them took a seat on a different matt.

"So mother or father?" Paul asked.

"Father. How'd you know?"

"For you to hide your ability for this long, you had to know from experience that it wasn't safe to reveal it. Was he Reader Force?"

Her breath caught in her throat. She nodded.

"Well, Lexy, I want you to look at these candles and pick one. Focus on the flame. Don't look at any of the other flames around it. Just look at that one. Let your vision blur and wander around that single flame so that it doesn't become uncomfortable, but don't look anywhere else."

She did as he asked. At first, her gaze wandered to the other flickering lights, but she kept her focus on one flame. Then Paul stood and moved a second candelabra behind the first. One by one, he lit the new candles.

"Keep focused," he said.

She shifted her gaze back to the first candle. With lights flickering behind the first row, it became more difficult to distinguish where each flame began and ended. But with extra willpower, she managed to keep her attention in one spot. Then he added a third row of candles and her eyes began to burn from focusing on that single flame for so long. Her vision was now filled with light. She put her hands on her temples and lowered her head, attempting to stay focused. With the fourth row of candles, she closed and rubbed her eyes. Spots of light stayed on her vision. She turned her head and opened her eyes, but all she could see was light.

"Good," he said. "Now we know your starting threshold. We can begin here and work our way up."

She looked back and found only three candelabras. The fourth was off to the side. Tendrils of smoke drifted from the recently blown-out candles.

"Now what?" she asked.

"When you're ready, I want you to focus back on that candle."

She closed her eyes and took a deep breath, then opened them and stared. Paul picked up the third row and moved the candles from side to side. The motion drew her attention, making it more difficult to remain focused on the stationary flame. He kept up the action until she lasted three passes without moving her eyes. Then he called Jared over and had him sway the second row while Paul continued to move the back row, in the opposite direction. Lexy stared and focused, but Jared's light was too distracting. Over and over, she looked at him. She rubbed her head and tried to clear her vision. After steadying her breathing, she opened her eyes to begin again. And so it went.

As she improved, Paul increased the difficulty. She kept focused on the single flame until it was all she could see. Then he called an end to the exercise. She blinked and looked up, shocked to realize the room was full of people. She rubbed her eyes and closed them, as much to ease the afterimage of the flames as to avoid looking at anyone. Without the focus of the candles, their energy was everywhere. Because they were much closer than the people outside, she felt the hum and pressure surrounding her.

"Breathe," Paul said.

She did and the pressure lessened. Turning her mind to Jared, she searched out his light and focused on that. The other pressures dropped away. Then she sought out Paul's energy, and it surged into her awareness. One by one, she shifted her mind to each of the people in the room, letting all the others drop away. For the first time in her life, she was controlling what she sensed and when. With a smile, she opened her eyes. Paul returned her smile and dismissed the others from the room. She took Jared's hand and he pulled her up.

Paul returned the candelabras to their original positions. "Realize that this will be more difficult outside the free zone.

But if you can focus your attention, you can learn to control your ability, even there."

"Thank you."

The church bell rang and people began filing out of the building.

"Where's everyone going," she asked.

"It's time for the Sunday feast." Paul walked with them to the door and followed them out.

All across their community, people were leaving their homes and walking to a large building connected to the back of the church.

"You're welcome to join us."

With her hand still in Jared's, Lexy followed. The building had thirty-foot high rafters. Wood double doors towered fifteen feet. Inside, ten long wooden tables stretched across the floor. Hundreds of lanterns lit the room. There was a performance stage. The musicians' had rested their instruments on their chairs as they sat at their own smaller table to eat. Lexy, Jared, and Paul sat on an elongated bench that ran along one of the tables, and were handed a bowl of fresh rolls and a dish of butter. The smell of the bread was enough to ease any of her tensions. Jared buttered a roll and handed it to her. The flavors were rich and creamy, unlike anything she could remember. Steam escaped as she tore open the bread. The butter melted on contact. Jared took another roll for himself.

"They get the butter fresh from the dairy," he said.

"This is wonderful." She took another roll with butter and scarfed it down.

Jared laughed.

More food dishes were passed down. Bowls of thick stew filled with cooked vegetables, meat, and broth. Every other plate had either steak, roast, bacon, or fowl. All the meat was seasoned and fell apart in her hands. They drank glasses of honey mead and ate their share of potatoes and corn. When she didn't think she could eat another bite, an assortment of cookies and cakes was passed down, bursting with molten chocolate or filled with nuts and berries.

After the last plate was passed, people walked behind the benches and carried the dirty plates away in open bins. Everyone stood and pulled the benches and tables back. The tables weren't actually ten long tables, as she'd first thought. Each one was made up of several smaller tables. They cleared the floor and the musicians took their seats. A man in a priest robe stood at the center of the stage and the room became quiet. Even the children were hushed and still.

"We thank God for seeing us through another good week and providing this meal for us to share." The man's voice carried even though he didn't have a microphone. "Now let us celebrate into the darkness, knowing he is always with us. No matter what the dawn shall hold, we have been blessed. So let it be as God wills it. Amen."

The crowd gave a united, "Amen," and applause. As the musicians played and the people dance,. Lexy felt their energy expand and brighten, as it had in the church service earlier that day. Silver sparkling lights danced in the air. It surrounded her without pressing in or suffocating her. She felt energized, excited, and jubilant. Her energy grew in response to the contact. She looked over at Jared and saw that his glow was brighter as well.

"Would you like to dance?" he asked.

She looked at the people on the floor. They were doing some kind of group dance she didn't know.

"I'll teach you." Jared took her hand and brought her to the edge of the crowd.

Standing behind her, he held her waist and helped her to move in time to the music. After a few passes of practice, he spun around to face her and continued to dance. He guided them sideways, then waited for an opening and pulled them into the group. Partners spun and danced around in a large circle. She stumbled a couple times, uncertain of tempo changes and confused when new moves were added, but Jared kept her going.

After a few songs, other people also helped her. A middle-aged woman in a red cotton dress showed her how to bow at the end of the song. A teenage girl in jeans and a tank top showed her the shuffle-and-spin move during one of the group-centered dances. Elderly couples dipped and waltzed, challenging her and Jared to do the same. Just like the homes and apparel, the music was a mixture of time periods and styles. Lexy laughed when she realized some of the tunes were adapted from songs she knew from the radio or clubs. They sounded strange being played with flutes and guitars instead of electric keyboards and synthesizers, but she kind of liked the change. This really was a place outside of history, with the best of every era preserved.

After a time, too much mead and all the Psy energy began to take their toll. Lexy became dizzy and stumbled into Jared. He guided her out into the night air. With his arm firmly around her, he led the way as she leaned her head against his shoulder. The sky was clear and the stars were visible. She thought of kissing his lips.

"Um, Lexy?"

"Hmmm?" She thought of kissing his broad chest and even lower.

"Lexy, you, ummm, wow, okay, um, you... you're pulsing, you know?"

"Hmm? What? Oh." She stepped back. "Sorry. I didn't mean to do that."

Jared cleared his throat and adjusted his pants. "Not a problem. At least now you know you can. I guess that means we share a strong connection. Come on." He pulled her in close and looked down at her. "I'll drive us back to the treehouse, and there we can... revisit this discussion."

She felt a fleeting touch inside her and melted into his embrace. Jared grinned.

He jumped and squirmed several times during the ride home. She tried to clear her mind, but the thoughts always led back to him. He finally stopped the car beside the lake and leaned over to grab her seat lever to push it back, then got on top of her.

"I'm going to have to teach you some more control techniques. But first..." He kissed her hard and grabbed her wrists. Pinned her down with his body and legs.

Then he let loose an onslaught of psychic fingers to explore every inch of her body. She didn't argue. After some of the things she'd imagined doing to him...

He sucked in a breath and she realized she had done it again. His sweet torture became more intense. She longed to move her hands and touch him back, but her mind did that for her. She felt him plunge inside her, and imagined covering him with her mouth, though his lips still physically covered hers. She was amazed by how real he felt. In her mind, her tongue and teeth raked down his shaft, even as his physical tongue moved in her mouth. She felt him move inside her lower regions, filling her with his entire length. Crying out against his mouth, she shook and grabbed his back, not with her real hands, but he felt it all the same. Then he was shaking, too. They breathed and kissed. He eased this grip on her wrists and she raised her hands to touch his back and hair.

"Now," He said as he pushed a hair out of her face and looking down on her with more love than she'd ever thought possible. "I'm going to teach you to control it."

"How?"

"Well..." he nibbled at her neck, sending shivers down her

spine. "I'm going to spend the rest of the night bringing you extreme pleasure."

"Hmmm, I'm liking this plan so far."

He chuckled. "Only, no Psy. Every time you pulse, I'm going to stop what I'm doing."

"That doesn't sound fair to you." She arched into his leg as he shifted his weight.

"Oh, you can do stuff to me, too. Just no Psy. Now, up to the treehouse." He opened her door and pushed off of her. "Time for your lesson.

8

L exy loaded a stack of papers into the scanner and sat down to wait for them to finish running through. She touched her band. Putting it back on was one of the hardest things she'd ever done, but as they drove closer to the city limits, she began to feel the pressure of uncontrolled Psy energy and knew she had no choice. Jared offered one of the disabled bands to her, but she still needed the active band. Even with it, her senses were heightened now. She was constantly distracted by people moving through the building, pulsing during their Psy session breaks, and the like. She tried to focus as she was taught the previous day, but it was difficult when all she wanted to do was leave this life behind and escape to the freedom of The Valley.

She took the papers from the output tray and saved the file on her computer, then saved another copy to her private flash drive. After checking for any other new files, she copied them over and ejected her USB. All these years she'd done this, she never knew what to do with the information. But something told her it needed to be saved, so she did it. Now she felt the time was finally right to do something. She still didn't know what that something was, but that would come.

Lexy remained quiet and let Kara do the talking on the ride home. She spoke of Curtis, at the exclusion of all other topics. Lexy grinned. Kara hadn't been angry that they were late to work today, which took her out of the running for her bonus Psy session. She didn't even mention it or how Lexy had spent the entire night away from their apartment. All she talked about was the day she had with Curtis and how she couldn't wait for the following weekend.

Lexy poured them both a glass of leftover birthday brandy and joined Kara on the couch.

"Do you ever wonder what life would be like if the bands were never invented?"

Kara paused her channel surfing and turned to face Lexy. "What do you mean?"

"I mean, what if everyone had learned to control their Psy energy without them. Sure, it would've taken some time, but then we wouldn't be slaves to bands and crystals. We could just be who we are."

"But Psy crime was too bad. They couldn't not have done something about that."

Lexy sighed and stood. She was tired of hearing that lie. It had cost her father his freedom. Ruined her family. Kept millions of people in slavery, year after year.

Kara stood and put a hand on her shoulder. Lexy felt the warmth of her glowing touch.

"Crime never went down after the bands. Criminals just found ways around them or went back to using their old methods. All the censorship and control didn't change anything. Crime actually went up, because they were rooting out and arresting all the police officers who knew how to fight it."

Kara took a step back, her hand still raised. "What makes you think all that?"

"My father was on the Reader Force. He saw it happen. And when he was of no further use to them, they took him away, too."

"Your father was a Reader?"

"And so am I."

"Oh, wow!" Kara put her glass down and paced. She turned off the TV and looked at it for a moment, then bent down and unplugged it. "That's why you never take off your band?"

Lexy nodded.

"Crime didn't go down?"

Lexy's heart skipped. "No."

Kara sat back on the couch and looked down at her clasped hands. "I don't know what to do with that." She brought her gaze back up. "If we tell anyone, they'll just arrest us." She lowered her head to her hands.

"That's assuming we could even get anyone to believe us if we did tell them."

"They wouldn't. Not without proof."

"What if there was proof?"

"Like what?"

"Like M.E. reports and their conflicting death certificates over the past twenty years."

Kara looked at Lexy with steel eyes. "You have that?" she whispered.

Lexy strode to her room closet and brought back a shoe box. After she sat next to Kara, she pulled out the flash drive from her pocket, opened the shoe box and dropped it in. There were dozens of other flash drives and SD cards already in there.

"I'm not sure if you're aware of this or not, but History Remembered keeps copies of all the documents we scan or transcribe. They're saved on a shared network which connects every data center in every state. It's their way of limiting the number of analysis agents they need. I got one of our local analysis clerks to tell me about it once. The people who actively censor the files are stationed in D.C. They access the records we save and make their changes before releasing the information to the public, but they never delete the old records. Those sit there in the archived files, untouched. I made a copy of everything. This is part of my collection of everything that's been censored or banned since the Storm. There are several other boxes. This is just my most recent."

"Okay, so you have the proof, but what do we do with it?" Kara's eyes were wide with panic, but she managed to keep her voice calm.

"I don't know. I wish there was some way to distribute it to everyone before it could be scrubbed. Not that I know if anyone would care. But even if people did care, what could they do about it?"

"They could choose to remove the bands." Kara reached up and took off her band, and her glow brightened. "They could choose to live without fear. We have to find a way to tell people."

Lexy hugged her friend as tears ran down her face. "You have no idea how happy I am to hear you say that."

Kara hugged her back and Lexy felt her warmth everywhere they touched.

"What about you?" Kara asked. "What about your band?"

Lexy sat back and swiped the wetness from her eyes. "I'm working on that. Jared's helping me."

Kara gave a toothy grin. "Oh, he's helping you, huh? Is that why you didn't make it home last night?"

Lexy play-slapped her roommate and giggled. "Yeah, well, I need a lot of help."

"I'll say." Kara sighed. "Please tell me you've at least gone Psy with him."

"Oh, we've done more than that."

"Syntercourse?" Kara's eyes widened.

"I'm not going to talk about that." Lexy got up.

"Oh, no you don't, Lexy Smith. You're going to sit your butt down and tell me every single sordid detail." Kara pulled her back down to the couch. "Is it really great? What about the risks? Is it worth it?"

"Why? Are you thinking about taking things to the next level with Curtis?"

Kara's cheeks flushed. "I don't even know if he would want to do something like that," she blubbered. "I mean, we haven't talked about any kind of commitment or exclusivity or anything."

"Then why didn't you go to the Psy sessions today."

Kara's face went blank. "How... how could you know that?"

"It's part of my gift." Lexy shrugged. "When everyone was gathered in the lounge, I felt that your Psy energy wasn't there."

Kara gasped, her eyes wide with fear. "You could feel where I was in the building?"

"Only because I know what your energy looks like. Otherwise, I wouldn't have been able to pinpoint it with my band on. There just isn't usually anyone on your side of the building during the afternoon session, so I got curious and looked closer. Besides, focusing on your energy helped to distract me from all the pulsing. But none of that's really important here. Why didn't you go?"

"I was about to, but the last one I went to this weekend wasn't much fun. My head wasn't in it. I couldn't stop thinking about Curtis. Afterwards, I just wanted to clock out so that I could go see him. And we had a great day yesterday. He took me to breakfast and then we spent the day at the zoo." Her eyes glowed. "I haven't been there since I was a teenager. We walked and rode the carousel, and we talked. We talked all day. I really like him. When we pulse... I don't know. It's different. I never knew it could be like that."

"There's a lot of things we never knew."

"So what do we do? How do we tell others without getting ourselves killed or thrown in jail?"

"I wish I knew. I've never been much of a planner."

"Then it's a good thing you have me. I happen to be an excellent planner. We're going to need a pen and paper, more brandy, and some chocolate."

Lexy grinned. "We don't have any chocolate."

"You might not, but I have a secret stash hidden in my room. You get the other stuff, and I'll be right back."

Kara swept back in the room a few minutes later, with a large box filled to the brim with snack cakes, candy bars, and other candies.

"Where did you get all this?"

"For years, I've been trading psygasms for chocolate."

They both picked out something from the box. Lexy refilled their glasses. Then they brainstormed a plan on how to change the world.

* * *

IT WAS ALMOST MIDNIGHT. The regulars ordered their last round and prepared to leave. The changeover would be happening soon. Jared helped Mick bus some tables and then waited at the bar. With Brian out for the next week, they would need all the help they could get. The recreational clubbers and experimental crowd always clogged the floor on weekends, but the Psy addicts turned out during the week.

"You should've seen her." Jared accepted a club soda. "She really came alive out there. Her face lit up. I swear, I could feel the energy she described. I wish I could see what she sees."

"You must really love this girl." Mick tilted his crocodile and cow leather hat at a couple of patrons as they stood to leave.

It was a movie replica complete with a row of crocodile

teeth around the front. He wore a matching leather vest, with a crocodile tooth necklace.

"Yeah, I do. I know how crazy that must sound since we just met."

"Nah. Brian was the same way. He proposed a week after they started dating. She said no. It was too soon. So he waited a week and tried again. After three months of that, she finally said yes. Brian was so shocked he knocked over a table, spilled all their food, and broke three dishes. He cut his hand so bad on the glass shards that they had to rush him to the doctor to get ten stitches. They got married two weeks later and have been together twenty years. Sometimes, crazy works."

The door to the back office opened and two men came out. They were dressed like everyone else in the bar, but their eyes gave them away. Information brokers, hiding in the club crowd. Brokers and suppliers came to see his father every night. Some even partook in some libations and pulsing to better fit in. Jared knew them by site, and these men were no exception. They worked for a company that developed herbal-based drug remedies, and stopped in at least once a week to schedule shipments to The Valley. They would slip out with the regulars and hurry to be out by twelve.

"Have the freezer boxes been switched?" Jared asked.

"Don't think so. You want to do it?" Mick handed him the key and lanyard from around his neck.

"Sure. I'll be right back."

The trays from the wall freezers in the men's bathroom had to be changed out twice a night. Because most ejaculation happened through Psy-sex, collection bags were worn to hold the fluids. When artificial inseminations became the norm, the state began the collection program to gather these bags and store them for future use. All night clubs and Psy dens were required to maintain proper freezer units to hold these bags until they could be turned in.

Jared turned the key and pulled out the freezer box full of bags. He transferred it to another freezer unit in one of the supply closets near the bathrooms. From there he brought back an empty box and locked it in the freezer. He checked the rack of empty bags and then went back out to the bar.

He tossed the key back to Mick. "Done."

"Good. Looks like the second wave's here."

A group of people in revealing attire and decked out in anti-crystals moved through the bar. Anti-crystals were costume jewelry made to resemble inhibitor crystals. Some years back, a claim was made that they increased Psy pleasure and intensity. Ever since, they became a fashion staple for the serious den rats. The group headed straight for the Dungeon—a dark dance room with stripper poles on short pedestals, lush velvet sofas lining the walls, and a cage people could enter to become the focus for everyone on the dancefloor. The cage sat on a platform over a wading pool made of glow-in-the-dark stone. A waterfall above the cage periodically splashed into the pool. Some more adventurous couples would engage in syntercourse in the cage.

The sound of the cage door rattling and water pouring down into the pool could be heard from the bar. resounded

"They're not wasting any time tonight," Mick said.

"Nope. You ever get tired of working here? Being around this, night after night?"

"Not really." Mick poured some drinks and passed them down the counter to a couple guys at the end of the bar. "If they want to go crazy and have Psy orgies every night, what do I care? That's their lives. It's none of my business any more than it should be their business if I want to settle down and have a family. At least here they have a safe place to do what they do with willing partners, and some degree of protection if they get in over their heads." He narrowed his eyes at the front door. "Like that one. Looks like a dare."

The young man walking in the club was probably under five-five. He didn't look that different than anyone else except for his height. He had a decent build and good coloring. But he appeared nervous. There was no excitement on his face. He touched his head where the band would normally sit, and flinched when he didn't feel it. Everyone had to take off their bands before they were let inside the club.

He drifted over to the bar and sat on a stool next to Jared. "Can I have something strong, please?"

"Sure thing." Mick poured a shot of whiskey and passed it to him.

The man gulped it with one toss back and put the glass back on the counter.

Mick poured. "First time Psy?" He poured a third shot.

"No. I mean, I've done psinterludes before. Just not used to so many people, is all. I'm usually one-on-one." The man already seemed more relaxed.

"What brings you in?"

"A girl." He grinned. "She's got this fantasy of the cage. A girlfriend of hers told her about it, and it's all she's talked about ever since. She said I can do whatever I want with her as long as it's in there."

A girl dressed in a thin white dress, with thigh-high white stockings and black ballet slip-on shoes walked in ahead of another wave of hardcore clubbers. Her hair was pulled up into two loose ponytails that fell down around her shoulders. She had sweet pink lips and wore pale blue eye shadow. She strode across the room to join the man at the bar and kissed him on the cheek. He brightened up.

"Can I get you anything?" Mick asked.

"Oh, no, I'm fine. Thank you." She pulled the man by his elbow and brought him to his feet.

He smiled and swiped his watch over the payment panel on

the bar. A beep signaled that the payment was accepted, and the two of them walked, arm-in-arm, to the Dungeon.

"Well," Jared pushed off the bar, "guess I better go keep an eye on our boy there, so he doesn't get pushed around too much by the hard cores."

"Be careful."

"I won't." Jared grinned.

The girl was already being helped into the cage by her boyfriend and a couple other people in the wading pool. Her eyes rolled and knees buckled as she stepped inside. Her boyfriend followed her in and the waterfall fell over them. People cheered and called out words of encouragement. The girl's thin dress was transparent. Hard nipples pushed against the wet fabric. She braced herself against the cage wall and stood with her legs spread open behind her. The boyfriend fumbled as he unhooked his pants and then pushed himself between her.

Jared turned his head, but the view around the room wasn't much different. Barely dressed women writhed on the poles. People kissed and Psy-played on the sofas. The dance floor was a moaning mass of frantic Psy-highs.

The girl in white shook and cried out in release. Her face was happy for a moment. Then it twisted in discomfort. Clearly not ready for the continued attention and non-stop pulsing, she tried to open the cage door, but some men from the crowd jumped into the pool and held the door closed. She screamed and fell to her knees. The men at the door cackled. Their eyes held thoughts of violence.

Jared attempted to push his way through the crowd, but it was thick. The girl was crumpled into a crying ball while her boyfriend beat at the cage, but the men wouldn't let go. Focusing his mind on the men, Jared pulled at their fingers and twisted them back. They jumped back and looked at the boyfriend, but he was as shocked as they were to see them hurt. He pushed at the door and knocked them into the water. Then after scooping up his girlfriend, he carried her toward the dancefloor, but the men in the pool rushed to grab his leg before he could exit the pool. A group of women helped the girl to stand and ushered her out of the room, while a fist fight broke out in the wading pool. Blood sprayed into the water. Some people ran into the bar. Some people cheered or jumped in. A few people kept doing what they were doing and ignored the whole thing. One man went to punch the boyfriend, but Jared psychically grabbed his arm long enough for the boyfriend to get in his punch first, which knocked the man out. Jared pulled at the feet of other men, making them lose their balance and fall into the water. One man hit his head on the side of the cage and knocked a tooth out as he fell.

With the crowd finally thinning, Jared was able to reach the pool. He pulled the boyfriend by the arm, but he didn't know friend from foe and tried to hit Jared, who blocked a punch by throwing up a Psy arm and dragged him away from the pool.

"Come on," Jared said. "Your girl needs you."

That was enough to get through to him. The boyfriend turned and bolted into the other room.

By this point, the two other bouncers had arrived. They helped Jared drag the men from the pool and throw them out of the club. By the time he went back in the Dungeon to drain the pool for cleaning, everyone was already dancing and pulsing again. He shook his head and went to check on the couple. Mick had taken them to a crystal room to recover. The girl looked up at Jared as he entered. Her eyes were full of fear, face covered in tears.

"I'm sorry I tried to punch you," the boyfriend said.

Jared help up a hand and shook his head. He knelt beside the girl and rubbed her hand. He thought about what Lexy had said. How when you wanted to comfort someone, a small amount of Psy energy transferred to that person would do the trick.

The girl began to relax.

"How are you feeling?" Jared asked.

"It hurts to breath. One of them... put pressure on my chest and lungs, while the others... I didn't know Psy-sex could hurt that much. They made it hurt." She sobbed on her boyfriend's shoulder.

Jared backed away and left them alone. He joined Mick just outside the room.

"She had bruises on her chest," Mick said, once the door was closed.

"That bastard would've killed her. I wish I'd known about the chest pain. I would've had him arrested for attempted murder instead of just throwing him out."

Violent Psy sex in a den or club wasn't against the law. It was generally accepted that you assumed a certain amount of risk and responsibility when going to those places. But clubs did have the freedom to refuse entrance to anyone who used their Psy pulses in an improper manner. If you wanted to play, you had to follow their rules.

"There's nothing that can be done about it now," Mick said. "You know how they are with pursuing Psy crime allegations when you don't have the suspect and no one actually got killed."

"They want to pretend it's all just a misunderstanding and leave it alone."

"Especially when you don't have a name and the guy looks like all our other clientele."

"I guess you're right. We don't want to draw too much attention to the club if we can help it."

They walked back up to the bar and Mick took back over for the bouncer, running the drinks.

"Did you have to pulse?" he asked.

"A few times. The crowd was pretty thick. It was hard to get to the pool."

"Did anyone notice?"

"I have no idea. There was a lot going on in there."

"Okay. Just be careful."

"I always am."

Mick snorted. "No, you're not."

"Well, I didn't figure you wanted the truth."

They laughed and went back to work. Jared checked on the boyfriend and girl several times, bringing them water and food to snack on. They finally emerged from the room an hour later. The girl looked much better, but she was still shaken. He saw them to the door and went back inside. When dawn arrived and the last patron was gone, he pulled the freezer box for storage and called it a night. He strolled back to his apartment, half-awake.

Jared became aware of being followed. He followed the shadows and felt his senses sharpen. One shadow reached up, and he ducked to avoid being stabbed. The three men from the pool circled around him on the sidewalk. He was only a few feet from the stairs to his apartment, but there was no way he could get inside before they reached him.

"I saw what you did," the leader said. "You're a Forcer."

Jared watched their muscle twitches and looked for an opening to call for help or run. "What are you talking about?"

"I saw you pull people back while you had your band on."

The leader paced around him, trying to put Jared's back to the wall and trap him. he stepped sideways instead, buying himself a few inches to maneuver in.

"I turned it off, genius."

"Well, it's set to *on* now."

"Your point?"

Two of the men lunged at Jared. He jumped back, but his leg still got caught by one of the men. He fell and the third man struck his stomach with a metal pipe, followed by a hit to the back of his head. They grabbed his arms and pulled him to his feet. Dragged him down to an alley one building down. He heard a groan and whimper, followed by shuffling. Struggling to clear his vision, he opened his eyes and saw the boyfriend and his girl tied up by a dumpster. The boy was unconscious but still breathing. The girl was awake.

"You like to play hero so much," the leader said. "What're you going to do now?"

Jared struggled against their hold and pulled one arm free. Twisting around, he threw one man to the ground and kicked another. The leader pulled the girl to her feet and held a knife at her throat. Jared stopped fighting. The men grabbed his arms again, this time gripping him tighter. The boyfriend stirred and opened his eyes. One look at the girl and he began struggling against his ropes, trying to stand.

"So what's it going to be?"

"What do you want?" Jared asked.

"I want you to admit you're a Forcer."

"And you think a confession born from holding a hostage and beating someone up three-on-one is worth anything? That's not going to hold up anywhere."

"You're right. A confession isn't worth anything. So how about a demonstration instead?" The leader grabbed the girl around her shoulders and tossed her into the street.

The sound of squealing tires echoed. This wasn't a wired road, so a driver would have to avoid the girl or run her over. In the split second it took to see that the driver wouldn't have the reflexes to turn, Jared did it for her. He pulsed, putting hands on the driver's, and pushing him to turn sharply. The car swerved and missed the girl.

"That'll do." The man smiled and motioned to his friends.

They hit Jared over the head a second time. Just before he lost consciousness, he heard them run away.

9

"I felt hands on mine," was the first thing Jared heard. Then, a girl crying.

He opened his eyes and pushed off the ground. A paramedic was examining the girl and tending to some scrapes on her arm. Her eyes were glazed and she had a cut and a bruise on her head.

A policeman was walking towards Jared. "Both of these men have bands on. Are you sure it wasn't someone else." The officer pulled the boyfriend to his feet and untied him.

The girl bawled as she threw the blanket from her shoulders and squeezed her boyfriend. The officer helped Jared to his feet and led him to the ambulance. Jared looked over at the club, but no one would be there now. Mick always took the back exit and left through an employee-only parking garage which was also used for special supplies transfers. They had a shipment going out that morning. Mick would've gone with it to make sure it reached The Valley safely, and Jared's father would be with him. They'd be gone most of the day, so Jared was on his own.

"Thank you for saving me," the girl said to him.

Her boyfriend's eyes widened and he shook his head to silence her.

The police officer narrowed his eyes at Jared. "Is your band working properly?"

"I... I don't know," Jared said. "I don't really use Psy all that much. They hit me in the head a couple times with some kind of pipe. Maybe they damaged it."

The driver of the car flicked his gaze over at him in panic, checking his Psy band, and asked if he could go. They let him. As he turned to walk away, Jared looked the man in the eye and saw an understanding there.

"We have to bring him in," another officer said. "It's procedure."

The first officer grabbed Jared's arm and led him into the police car. Jared looked at the badge and thought of Lexy's father. *How many good people had he been forced to arrest, to protect his family.*

The officers took the front seats and looked back at him nervously, through the bars separating them. He sighed and looked out the window, at the stairs to his apartment as they drove away.

Once they reached the stations, the original two officers were replaced by men in suites with strange looking inhibitor bands and crystals everywhere. They had crystal buttons on their jackets, crystal cufflinks, crystal-encrusted watch phones, and crystals lining their bands. The next several hours was a series of questions and electric shocks to provoke reactions. He maintained his control, even when the electrical charges grew stronger. In his mind, he fortified a wall between things he was allowed to confess under torture and things he must never reveal. At some point they would provoke a reaction. Either through sleep, food deprivation, dehydration, or pain, they would break him. But he couldn't reveal the ones who knew his secret or the work his father did. And he couldn't say anything about Lexy. Couldn't let them find her. With that in mind, he let them do what they would.

* * *

LEXY SAT STRAIGHT UP. Her heart was pounding, but she didn't know why. *Must've been a bad dream.*

It took her a moment to remember why she was in the living room instead of her bed. She was curled up on the loveseat. Kara snored softly on the couch. Their notes, empty glasses, and candy wrappers were on the coffee table. Lexy put her feet on the plush carpet. Cool air moved her hair as the air conditioner kicked on. Sunlight streamed through the curtains and highlighted dust particles in the air. Everything was quiet. Her heart was still drumming, but she couldn't remember anything from her dream. Couldn't remember dreaming at all. The alarm clock on her watch beeped. She hit the silence button and saw that it was already thirty minutes past her normal wake-up time. She and Kara had slept through the beeping six times.

"Kara."

Her friend mumbled something and turned over.

"Kara," she called louder.

"What?" Kara rubbed her eyes and pushed up on to her elbows.

"We overslept. We're late for work."

"Oh, is that all? We've both got like a dozen sick days. Just email HR for both of us and go back to sleep." She laid her head back down and turned onto her side. "How late were we up last night anyway?" Her eyes were still closed.

"I don't know. Two o'clock, maybe."

"And we still couldn't come up with a plan." Kara yawned and blinked. Then she snapped her eyes open "Are you okay?" She sat up and leaned over to Lexy. "You look pale and sick.

Was it all the chocolate or the drinking? Do you need some water or something?" She hopped up and went to the kitchen, then brought back a glass of water and handed it to Lexy.

She accepted the water but didn't drink. "I don't feel sick."

"Then what's wrong?"

"I don't know. My heartbeat won't slow down. I feel like something's wrong, but I don't know what."

"You want me to call someone? What about Jared?"

Lexy thought of Jared and reached for her watch phone. Then a feeling of dread and horror swept through her.

"I can't call him."

"Why not?"

"I don't know."

"Lexy, you're freaking me out. I'm calling Curtis." She rushed into the kitchen and whispered into her phone.

After hanging up, she hurried back into the living room and put a hand on Lexy's leg. She was still sitting like that when Curtis knocked on their door thirty minutes later.

Sorrow overtook Lexy and all she could think about was Jared, their future together, and the overwhelming certainty that she would never see him again.

10

T he only thing Jared could think about was Lexy. They covered his eyes and ears with a sensory deprivation helmet and moved him on some kind of stretcher. If he didn't know where they were, he couldn't pulse at them. A blindfold would be sufficient ninety percent of the time. Nearly everyone needed to see who they were influencing, but there were a few infamous Forcers in the early days who were able to locate a person by sound and hurt them. Since he still hadn't reacted to any of their interrogations, they had no idea how strong he was.

The helmet also kept him from knowing where they were taking him. Time warped with no outward cues. Jared focused on his sense of touch and smell. He could smell the deodorant and shampoo of the people around him. He could feel the movement of the fabric when they touched his bed. The way his body swayed and shook, he knew they were moving him by vehicle, but he couldn't tell how far. When they talked, sometimes he felt the vibrations through the stretcher's metal rungs. He imagined what they were saying about him. *What'll they do next?*

The men in suits weren't happy when he didn't react as they'd expected. He managed to keep his powers under control even when the electric shocks and beatings left him weak and disoriented. He felt like vomiting. He wanted to sleep, but the pounding of his heart and blood rushing through his ears was distracting.

The stretcher stopped and the smells disappeared. He was alone, but where? They left him tied to the bed. With the helmet, fatigue, and hunger pains, he probably would've fallen and hurt himself if he had tried to move around. He kept opening his eyes, wishing for a speck of light. His eyes played tricks on him, seeing light where there was none. As he examined the darkness, he wondered why he'd never noticed the complexity of it? It wasn't a solid color, but a nebula of black and dark gray. At times, he could see colors hidden in the blackness.

Then he noticed a speck of light. He thought it was another trick of his eyes. He blinked, but the light remained. His eyes and mind focused on it, and it grew brighter in response. His mind drifted again to thoughts of Lexy and the light flared. His heart sped up. Was this the light Lexy saw in people? Was he seeing her? He pictured her face and thought of touching her cheek, and the light flared again. He put his fingers through hers and squeezed them. The contact felt real, but with his mind on the verge of breaking, he couldn't be sure. It could've been a hallucination borne out of madness and fear. Even if he could reach her from however far apart they were, he had no idea if she could sense him without removing the band. But the contact felt real, and that was all he had.

Taking comfort in the feel of her hand in his, he called out to her, told her he loved her. He prayed she would be safe and warned her to be careful. Then he pulled away.

She said she could see a person's pulse. There could be others like her who could follow his contact back to Lexy. He couldn't take the chance of leading anyone to her. He saw the speck of light dim again, and his heart ached, but it had to be done. He had to protect her. He squeezed his eyes shut, trying to ignore the one spot of light in all the darkness.

Time lost all meaning again. He focused on the pulse in his head and flexed his fingers, putting small amounts of pressure against his bonds. He could feel the strength returning to his muscles. He thought out various plans, but none seemed good enough. If he fought, which would reveal his Psy strength, and managed to escape, they would go after his father and friends. If by some miracle he could wait them out, maybe they'd give up and believe he'd told the truth about not being a Forcer. Of course, they would kill him then. They couldn't allow him to tell the world how he'd been treated. It would be a scandal that would threaten their control over the people.

Escaping without using any Psy powers was the best option. But he had no idea where he was being held or what kind of defenses the building had. There was still a chance his father would find him and come after him, but that could get them all killed. The best thing he could do was wait and be ready to act when the time was right.

He smelled vanilla perfume. Cold fingers and long nails touched his face. There was a click and the helmet was released. Jared blinked at the sudden light and tried to look at his surroundings. He felt lightheaded. A man dressed in scrubs leaned over and unhooked his arms. Jared was helped down from the stretcher and allowed to sit in a chair beside a square white table. A woman in a black mini-skirt and business jacket buttoned at the waist, revealing a silk camisole top, stood by a chair on the other side of the table. She stared at Jared. Her nails were painted dark red, matching her lips. Her eyes were painted with dramatic brown and black lines. Black hair was pulled back into a bun at the base of her neck. Gold studs in her ears. Nowhere on her was any hint of crystal jewelry. The only protection she'd worn was her inhibitor headband. She removed it and put it between them on the table before taking her seat. The man in scrubs moved back to the door, behind the woman, and Jared felt his mind clear. The man was a Shield. Jared could work through a Shield, but they did leave him feeling a dizzy afterwards. Thankfully, Brian could extend or retract his nullification field, or Jared wouldn't have been able to spend much time with him.

"So no crystals?" Jared said. "Does that mean you guys have finally figured out that you were wrong about me?"

The woman sat back, still watching him with piercing eyes, and crossed her legs. "Here's what we know. You were wearing a non-functioning inhibitor band in public, which is against the law. In addition, you were observed using Psy ability on banded individuals."

"I don't know what those people saw, but it must've been someone else."

She removed a silver watch phone from her coat pocket and turned it on. He recognized the scuff marks on the screen and worn-off paint on the side buttons.

With a few clicks, she pulled up his contact list and scrolled through it. "Perhaps one of your friends will be more knowledgeable."

She called out names of people he worked with, old high school contacts, the person who tailored his pants, vendors who supplied items for the Den, and random people. Some of them he didn't even recognize anymore.

"Lexy Smith," she said.

Jared kept his face expressionless.

She glared at him again with her piercing eyes. "Lexy Smith. Who is that woman to you?'

"That's just some girl I met last week. We went out to a club together. I hardly know her."

"That's not what your energy is telling me."

His chest constricted.

"That's right. I'm a Reader. So why don't we start over. You are a Forcer. How far can you pulse?"

"I don't know. I've never measured it."

"Guess."

"Thirty feet maybe."

That was about how far away he was from the car. If he'd said any less than that, she'd know it was a lie.

"Prove it. In the next room, to your right, there are five people. I want you to touch them. Nothing fancy, just enough that they feel it."

"I can't see them."

"Humor me. There's one at each of the four corners and one in the center of the room. The dimensions of the room are the same as this one. Now pulse."

Jared contemplated pretending to pulse, but Lexy had said she could see when a person pulsed and who it was directed to. So he focused on the places the woman had indicated and imagined touching the five people on the shoulder. The woman smiled.

There was a knock at the door and another man in scrubs looked in. "They each reported feeling a hand brush across their shoulder."

"Thank you," the woman said.

The man closed the door and disappeared.

"Now I want you to kill one. Your choice."

"What? You're crazy."

"If you're worried about killing an innocent person, I assure you, they're all criminals."

"According to you people, so am I." Jared shook his head. "I'm not a killer."

"We'll see." The woman put her on band and left.

Once the door was closed, the Shield approached Jared and held up the helmet. "If you struggle, I'll put you back on the stretcher and strap you down. If you put this on without a problem, you can keep your arms and legs free."

After glancing around to memorize his surroundings, Jared allowed the man to put the helmet back on.

* * *

"Should we do something?" Curtis whispered.

"Like what?" Kara furrowed her brow and splayed her hands. "She hasn't said a word in over an hour."

"Well, I've already checked his apartment and his father's club. No one's there. If she won't let me call him, I don't know what to do."

"Oh, don't even mention calling him again. I could barely get her to stop shaking and crying the last time we suggested it."

Lexy heard them talking but didn't remained motionless on her bed. She squeezed her pillow into her chest and pressed her chin into it. She was cold from the air conditioner but didn't pull the covers up. They'd led her into her room shortly after Curtis arrived, and now her friends stood just inside the doorway. She didn't look at them, but she could see their energy all the same. His body gave off a warm glow as he tried to calm and comfort Kara.

Lexy closed her eyes when she felt a touch on her cheek. She opened them again. Her mind searched for Jared, but the feeling was faint. She felt his hand on hers and let the tears pour out. Kara rushed to her side. Lexy clung to the transparent ribbon of Psy energy connecting her to Jared. She followed it back to him, but he was far away. She felt his desperation and love for her. He was afraid and worried for her safety. She could feel that he was hurt or had been recently, but he was holding back thoughts of the pain. Even now, he was maintaining his control, trying to protect her. Tears streamed down her face.

She tried to tell him she was coming for him, that she would find a way to help him, but she didn't know if he could hear her or what she would even do.

Then the contact was gone. He pulled back, afraid of revealing her to the people who held him. She sat up and tore off her inhibitor band, focusing in on the speck of his light with all her willpower. She wouldn't lose him again. Upon expanding her awareness around him, she saw other people nearby and mentally noted everything. Any detail could tell her where he was. Pulling back again, she looked for concentrations of people and areas where there weren't many lights. A picture gradually formed in her mind. She dashed to the living room to grab the sheets of loose paper left over from the previous night, and sketched what she saw, including notes about how far apart things might be and how many people she sensed in each area. She drew out every detail she sensed from the place he was being held. She couldn't see buildings or other structures, but she could got a sense of how tall a building was by how people were spaced above and below each other.

By the time Lexy finished, she was shaking again. As she moved her focus away from her work, she became aware of all the Psy energy around her. Light flooded her vision. She swayed in her seat and would've fallen, but someone caught her and put her inhibitor band in her hand. She pulled it on and leaned back against the sofa, with a sigh of relief. With all the other lights dimmed, she could close her eyes and once again focus on the tiny bead she knew to be Jared.

Kara sat beside her.

Curtis looked over her drawings. "This looks like a map of the county. This empty strip is the same shape as the river, and everywhere you have a lot of people is about where the cities would be in relation to the river. But what's that up near the top?"

The afterglow of light was still too bright to see well, but she didn't need to open her eyes to know what Curtis was referring to.

"That's the building where Jared is."

"Did he show this to you?"

"How could he show it to her?" Kara scrunched her face.

Lexy opened her eyes to meet her friend's gaze. "Jared is a Forcer."

Kara looked over at Curtis, who nodded while looking down and away. She opened her mouth and closed it again. There was a fear at knowing the band didn't work against him and he could touch her whenever he wanted. Lexy knew that fear. She'd felt it, too, when Curtis told her the truth. But Jared hadn't abused his power. And if Kara really did want to live in a world without bands, as she'd claimed last night, whether or not someone was a Forcer should be a non-issue.

Kara relaxed and nodded.

Lexy turned back to Curtis. "And no, he didn't show this to me. He didn't have to. I'm a Reader."

"Is that why you can't stand to take your band off? Never mind. That's not important right now. Does this mean you know where he is?"

"From what I could see when he contacted me, there were people on at least ten floors around him."

"Ten floors?" Curtis said. "There's only one building in a hundred miles that tall."

The Fixton building in Marks was the tallest building in the area. On paper, it was a research facility. But everyone knew it was more than that. There were rumors that it was a political prison. No one spoke of that in polite circles, but they all knew about it.

"He's been arrested," Lexy said.

"What do we do?" Kara asked.

Lexy looked at her friends. She knew she would go after Jared, but it was almost a certainty that she would get arrested or killed in the process. *Why didn't I tell him how I felt about him when I had the chance? He could die now. We both could die, and I never said I loved him.*

She looked down at her reflection in the glass coffee table. The silver of her inhibitor band reflected light from the window, and she remembered the day her father brought home the bands. Her mother was relieved. They would be safe. Lexy would be able to hide her abilities, unlike her father. They pretended this would fix everything, but it was already too late for him by that point. Her parents never spoke of it in front of her, but she heard the hushed conversations and half-sentences they were too afraid to complete. She felt when they lied to her or each other. They were trying to protect her. She understood that, even as young as she was. Her father hated the band. His senses had saved his life multiple times. He didn't see the logic in dulling them. *"It gets easier and it's worth it,"* he'd told Lexy. *"It's who we are."* Her father would be ashamed of her.

She snatched off her band. Ignoring the protests of concern from Kara, she let the light surround her. Lexy clenched her head while doubled-over in her seat, taking slow even breaths. Her father had learned to live with the light at a time when no one wore the bands. How much brighter and more confusing must it have been for him?

"Kara, please go to my mother. Bring her somewhere safe."

"Where can we go?"

"I know a place," Curtis said. "What about you? Are you planning to go after him alone?"

Lexy lazily opened her eyes, still holding her head. "I'll go in after nightfall. That should give me enough time to watch their security patterns, I hope. When the Den opens, tell Jared's father what happened and take him these." She picked up the box of data cards from under the table, at her feet. "I have a few more in my closet. Hopefully he can figure out some way to distribute this information."

"What's in here?"

"The truth." Lexy stood, finally feeling steady. "Kara can explain more. I have to go."

"Wait." Kara rushed to her bedroom and came back with a fashion hat.

It was bowled and had a hard rim, like something that might've been worn a hundred years before.

"If you're going out unchained, you'll need something to hide your head."

Lexy turned the hat over, but there was no band on the inside. Most hats were either made with enough room to wear above the bands or had inhibitor bands built in.

"It's old," Kara said. "Used to be my grandmother's."

"Thank you." Lexy looked up at her and was struck by the swirls of pinkish purple and royal blue swimming through her light.

Her eyes had a lavender glow, and even though Kara's band was also off, the vibrations of her energy didn't overwhelm Lexy. Instead, a soothing warmth radiated from her. Lexy hugged her and the warmth spread through her body. She felt encouraged and hopeful. There was no way she should be able to succeed, yet she had faith that she would. Somehow, by the grace of God, she would be with Jared again.

11

J ared stared into darkness and began to lose hope. He shuffled around, feeling everything within reach. Several times, he felt he was being watched. The temperature in the room repeatedly changed from warm to cold and back. He counted the seconds and found that the cold air would blow for five minutes, followed by ten minutes off. The pattern repeated four times and he decided it must be on a set cycle. Now he could track how much time passed, which was a huge elevation to his state of mind.

He sat on his bed and went over what he knew of his room. Thirty steps to the door and thirty two steps wide. From his bed, five steps right and two forward to the sink and toilet. The table and chairs were twenty steps to the left of the sink and five steps across. From there, it was five steps back and ten to the side to return to the bed.

After he'd walked the floor a hundred times, counted several hours by the change of the air conditioner, and drove himself into mental exhaustion from repeating how many steps it took to get to every spot in the room from any spot in the room, Jared rested on his bed and tried not to think about the dark silence. On the periphery of his senses he saw Lexy's light. It took great force of will not to reach out to her. Their brief contact earlier was the one thing keeping him going. He knew she could still sense him, and he knew she would sense it if he died. He had to stay alive for her.

Then, during the ten minutes of warmth, he felt a draft of cool air coming from the direction of the door. He waited, muscles tensed, but it didn't prepare him for the sudden pain in his stomach. It felt like a fist with a ring on one finger. Jared rolled to his side and fell off the bed. He landed on his ankle and knees and felt around, trying to find his attacker. The second hit was just as unexpected. And it continued. He was hit in the back, kicked in the stomach with what felt like pointed steel-toed shoes, slammed across the back, and smacked across the kneecaps. Every hit came from a different direction and was followed by several moments of nothing, so he didn't know where his attacker was.

Then it stopped. Jared remained still for many heartbeats. The rush of air from the A/C kicked on. He wanted to walk the room, to know he was alone, but it would be nothing to try to stay ahead of a man who couldn't see or hear. Walking the room would prove nothing. So he went back to his bed and waited.

The next time he felt the rush of air from the door, he made a run for it. He had no weapon, no eyes or ears, and no knowledge of the building past his room. The mystery attacker slammed him into the wall, and he felt a rib crack. Then the beating resumed. In between coughing up blood and clutching his stomach, he caught a scent of soap or perfume. After sending out a pushing pulse in the direction of the scent, he was rewarded with contact. There was a pause. Then the air from the door stopped. His attacker was gone.

Jared stayed on the floor for two rounds of the air conditioner before pulling over to the sink and attempting to clean up. His initial feeling of relief and achievement was gone. There was no success to be had from using his pulse as he had. This was what the woman had wanted, to see what he would do when hurt, and he'd fallen for it. Then again, what was he supposed to do? His chest hurt from the rib break and he could barely put any weight on his ankle.

He turned off the sink and hobbled back to his bed. While focusing on Lexy's light, he fell asleep.

* * *

"Looks like she finally caught a strong one," the old man said.

Logan agreed. It was always difficult to watch when they caught any new prisoner. In the early days, they would be tortured until they agreed to work for the government. Those who didn't were tossed into the lower cells. It wasn't so bad there. They were mostly forgotten. But as the years wore on, the torture of new captures became different. As a Reader, Logan was able to observe the change in each prisoner's Psy energy as the strange experiments took place. Only he and a few other Readers were strong enough to understand what was going on. The others were either too weak to begin with or their abilities had degraded from disuse and apathy. They could see past a few dozen feet at best, and most didn't care what they saw when there was something within their range.

But Logan watched and listened. His greatest secret was his knack for picking out stray thoughts along the Psy pulses. Only the old man had confessed to a similar skill. They watched as *she* set things in motion for this new unlucky soul. He was strong. Logan felt him pulse once, far beyond the confines of the buildings. Even now, there was a faint connection there, though he wisely avoided any further active contact with this person he obviously cared for.

Logan saw him touch the people he couldn't see, and he felt

Val's energy buzzing with joy. She had been waiting for one like him, someone who could pulse without their senses. It was the ultimate achievement for weapon development. While Psy abilities gave assassins the freedom to kill without touch, they still needed to be close enough to see or hear their target. If you could train someone to kill without those restrictions, it opened the door to a wide range of options. Find a Forcer with some range who was skilled enough to do so and the options were limitless.

"She isn't holding anything back this time." Logan said.

He felt sorry for the man. From what he could hear through the Psy energy in the building, this one was caught while saving a life. He had a good energy, and he'd refused her requests to kill, which had cost him greatly. Val was ruthless when it came to provoking the reaction she wanted. And she was successful. Unlike any of her previous prisoners, this man had learned to attack what he couldn't see. The beatings would only grow more severe, until he was pushed to the point where he must choose to kill or die. Then self-preservation would likely win over and he would kill his attacker. What he couldn't know was that his attacker was someone like him, a prisoner tortured to the point of submission, forced into the same choice to fight or die.

Logan screwed his face. He'd always hated Val, even before the Storm. He never trusted her. She wore a shield, like him, and they were supposed to stick together, guard each other's backs. Trust should've been a given, but he never felt right about her. Her eyes were absent of light. The Storm only confirmed his suspicions. She hid behind her shield and played by the rules, but she never did so to serve or protect anyone.

He forgot about her, at first. There was a lot of adjustments to be made and much to deal with. Old hatreds were forgotten. Everyone began anew, on a clean slate as they struggled to get a handle on their new senses. His connection with her was even strengthened once he realized they had something in common. The two of them saw the light and few others could. New teams were developed, and they began to work and train together more frequently. Then came the Purge. She used the information she'd learned while pretending friendships, and helped the State develop false cases against each Reader on the Force. Val played them against each other. None of them knew how skilled she was at that game. She learned their fears, knew their families, and hit them where it hurt. One at a time, they were killed or brought to Fixton. As far as any of them knew, only Tracy Lin had escaped, but not without a cost. Val killed Tracy's husband and sister to frame and arrest her former teammate. No one believed Tracy when she accused Val of the crime. — Tracy's husband was killed with Psy and everyone on the force knew that Readers had trouble pulsing. While Tracy shared a close enough connection to him to commit the crime, experience indicated that Val shouldn't have been able to accomplish the thought-killing. Logan was the only one who believed her back then. Now everyone in the prison knew she was right. Val could pulse. Not as strong as a non-Reader, and her range was limited to only a few feet, but it was enough to get the job done. What she didn't account for was Tracy's little brother. As the manhunt grew fierce, her brother awakened to his ability as a Shield and hid his remaining sister from their pursuit. They'd been in hiding ever since.

Logan shook off the memories and tossed a piece of bread over to the old man. They ate the meager meal in silence. The old man, once a captain at another precinct, had transferred to their group in the early days when they were still recruiting skilled Readers to develop plans and solve crimes. One of the patrolmen, a non-Reader named Tom, came through the pen that first night after he arrived and asked who the old man was. Tom was mortified when the old man walked up and introduced himself with a smile, but he wasn't the least bit insulted. He said he may be old, but that just meant he'd been smart enough to survive that long. He considered it an honor to earn that title. All of them began calling him Old Man from that point on. Of course, he was only in his mid-forties at the time. Now he really was an old man.

"Logan, do you see anything different about that light the boy is watching?"

Logan leaned back and followed the trail. It was now coming strongest from the person on the other end. Whoever the Forcer was connected to was keeping the connection open despite his efforts to close it. At the end of the trail was a sparkling light obscured by haze and distance.

"I can't tell much. The person is too far away."

"She is far. I'll give you that. But if I can see her, then you should be able to as well."

"You can see her?" Logan pushed his focus to the person at the other end of the thread.

Whoever she was, she was getting closer. That meant she also had to be a Reader. For her to see her friend at that distance, she had to be a strong one, but Logan couldn't see any more than that. He looked around at people near her, but they were clear, so the distance wasn't the issue as he'd first assumed.

"I can't see her," Logan said.

"I figured as much, which can only mean it's an Oedipus block."

Logan's eyes widened. An Oedipus block was the natural phenomenon whereby closely related family members were unable to affect each other psychically due to the similarity in their Psy energy frequency. Readers could still see near kin, but it was hazy and they couldn't psychically touch or communicate with one another. Generally, the block was stronger on the side of the child than the parent, with parents having a greater sense of their offspring than vice versa. The block could grow weaker with time and practice, but it never disappeared.

Logan put his head down. "No. She can't come here."

"I don't see how you can stop her," Old Man said. "You can't communicate with her. She probably can't even sense you're here, no matter how strong she's become. She's coming for him, and based on the strength of that connection, I don't see that there's anything that would stop her."

"Val will see her the minute she gets anywhere close to this building. I have to find a way to help her." Logan stood and paced the room.

There was a stirring once the other men and women of the cell noticed their conversation and began mumbling about his agitation. He knew his energy was flaring and struggled to put a clamp on his thoughts and emotions before it could be noticed outside of their room. "

What's going on?" one of the men asked.

"His daughter," Old Man said. "She's on her way here, now."

Logan felt a wave of energy pass through the room and turned to look back. Everyone was standing and looking at him, with compassionate expressions and vibrating in their hearts. He looked at Old Man, who stood and smiled.

"So what's your plan?"

LEXY STRUGGLED with the steering wheel, but the road was full of holes and uneven breaks. Each one threatened to run her off into the grass or down the sidewalk. These roads hadn't been used in a long time. There weren't even any open businesses or homes along most of the route. She was too far from the wired roads. The area was abandoned, in favor of consolidating everything at a central location. It would've been faster to drive the wired roads, but it was also easier to be tracked that way. If someone saw her car going too far from its regular destinations, they could start asking questions. This would be especially true if she was already being pinged for her connection to Jared. If they really wanted to find her, they still could, but traveling off the wires could buy her some time.

Signs of life started cropping up. It began with a lit window or random car driving by. People sat on building steps and walked home from bus stops. Music played from bars and clubs. Pedestrian traffic grew thicker. People walked across the street, in front of her car, without a second glance. Some didn't even give a first glance. They moved like they owned the streets and she was the one who needed to get out of the way.

Lexy rubbed her forehead to ease her band withdrawal headache. As the amount of people increased, so did the Psy energy. And most of people around there weren't banded, nor were they adept at controlling their energy. Some of the clubs were intense bright. The businesses weren't crystaled, so any Psy activity from within their walls could be seen and felt from miles away. She kept her head low and eyes diverted and continued driving.

Then she ran over one pothole too many and her car swerved from the force of the blown tire. She maneuvered her car to the side of the road and turned off the engine. A few people turned to look at her, then went back to what they were doing. She popped the trunk and tucked her keys in her pocket, then got out to retrieve her spare tire. After pushing past the junk, she lifted the flap and pulled out her spare and tools. It didn't take long to prop up the car and get the flat tire off, but the dummy tire took a few tries to get tight enough. All the while, she kept her senses trained for anyone who may approach her. Thankfully, she was left alone. After tossing the flat in her trunk, she got back in the car and drove.

Having to drive slow on her dummy tire and over the bad roads, it took another half-hour before she reached the city limits. Upon feeling the lag of another flat tire, she pulled over to the nearest business and looked around. There was more traffic. Some people looked like locals, and there was a fair number of homes within walking distance, but there were also a lot of cars from the city. People in nice suits and dresses walked by people in dirty, torn clothing and bare feet. The streets were lined with bars, clubs, theaters, and artists. About half the people wore inhibitor bands. Psy energy was every-where, and vibrations hit her from all directions. The buildings were old, but not without some charm. Wire railings and posts formed balconies which were home to dancers and diners alike. Just like the earlier clubs she'd passed, the buildings here weren't protected by crystals and she could see the Psy outlines of people dancing and moving provocatively. Other people were simply drinking or eating. Psy-sex houses were tucked behind the front row of businesses, not visible to normal sight but close enough for her to get a read on. Ahead of her, a group of loud women roamed the streets and weaved in and out of clubs. They wore feathered boas, strings of lights, and reeked of alcohol. They appeared to be enjoying bachelorette cele-brations.

Back before the Storm, women would throw a party before getting married. Now, with marriage nearly extinct in the city, women still yearned for a reason to celebrate and party with their friends. They missed the tradition, so some women would throw annual bachelorette parties, not to celebrate getting married, but to celebrate their continued status as a bache-lorette.

Trying her best to ignore everything, Lexy searched around and saw the outline of the Fixton building a few blocks away. After locking her car and adjusting her hat, she strode in that direction.

12

Curtis waited for the any signs of life at the Den. The club didn't open for a couple hours, but that didn't mean someone wouldn't show up before that. Kara and Lexy's mom waited in the backseat. No one said a word. Finally, a light went on and he saw someone walk by the window. He hopped out, locked the doors and hurried to the club's front door. It took ten knocks before someone answered.

A man wearing a black laced-up renaissance-style shirt and brown leather pants answered the door. He had on tall cuffed boots and a sheathed dagger at his hip.

"You must be Mick."

The man looked over Curtis, then noted the car sitting across the street. "And you are?"

"Curtis. I'm a friend of Jared's. He's in trouble."

Mick stepped back and let him in. Showed him to the back of the room, down a long hall. Knocked on a door marked *Traymore* and waited for the man in the room to answer. Then he opened the door and walked in, motioning for Curtis to follow.

The resemblance of man behind the desk to his son was clear, even if Curtis hadn't recognized the name on the door.

They had the same sharp nose, dark red brown hair, and cut of the jaw. Even their mannerisms were similar. This was definitely Jared's father.

"Can I help you?" Traymore asked.

Mick stepped to the side to allow Curtis to speak.

"Jared's been arrested."

The two men shared a glance.

"And you know this because?" Traymore asked.

"His girlfriend told me. She's... got strong senses. She's a Reader. This morning, she went near catatonic and said she sensed him at Fixton. Told me to come see you and bring you these." Curtis handed over a handful of cards from his pocket. "She's got hundreds of these in boxes. They have copies of everything that's been censored since the Storm. For some reason she thought you could do something with them. She also asked me to get her mom to safety. I know Jared spoke about some safe place near here, but he never showed me where it was. I was hoping you could see that she got there."

Traymore handed the cards to Mick, who pulled up a laptop.

"It seems legit," Mick said, after checking a couple cards and a flash drive. "There's books on here I haven't seen since high school, and I saw some unedited police reports and public records files on the flash drive. How did she get this?"

"She works for History Remembered. Apparently, she's been copying all their files for years. She didn't even tell her roommate about it until last night."

Traymore turned back to Curtis. "And where is she now?"

"She went after Jared earlier today."

"She went after him by herself? What hope does she think a recently unchained Reader has against a prison full of trained Psy guards?"

"She was determined. That's why she asked me to take care

of her mom. She's afraid that if she gets caught, they might go after her."

"A wise concern," Mick said. "What should we do, sir?"

Traymore stood and walked over to a metal filing cabinet. He took out a handwritten address book and handed it to Mick.

"See to the girl's mother, then gather all these data cards and distribute them to the printers. Contact everyone on the list and tell them it's time."

"Sir?" Mick's body tensed.

"We've been waiting for a sign. It doesn't get any bigger than this. Everyone knows what to do, and this uncensored information is the goldmine we've been waiting for. Besides, if she really is going to try a prison break, she'll need a distraction. If we can get things moving fast enough, it could give her a chance. And if we're lucky, her prison break plan will serve as a distraction for us as well. We can attack them on both fronts." Traymore pulled his keys from his desk drawer and headed to the door. "I'm counting on you to run this like we planned."

"Where will you be?" Mick followed him out into the hall.

Traymore opened the backdoor, which led to the parking garage, before turning back to Mick and putting a hand on his shoulder.

"I'm going after my son."

And then he was gone.

* * *

It didn't take long to make all the calls. Mick only had to do the first thirty, and they all knew their roles, so no explanation was required. Those thirty called the rest of the massive phone tree. Within a half-hour, three thousand people had been contacted. Within an hour, that number would've tripled.

The first string was the priests, ministers, and rabbis, who informed their congregations. They would coordinate peaceful band-free demonstrations throughout this city and in all other cities in the state.

The tech guys would make sure that every printer in every home produced copies of uncensored texts, arrest warrants and court rulings from police officers who'd been wrongfully imprisoned since the Storm, and every crime that was covered up. These documents would also be posted on the Internet. Any 3D printer would be sent commands to create sports equipment and other banned items. Every tablet or television with Internet access would be sent images of old movies and clips from once popular sporting events. Hackers would broadcast live feeds of every protest.

Then came the teachers. With most children abandoned to State-run foster care schools, the underground movement knew how important it was to put people in place there. Up until now, the role of their undercover teachers had been to counteract the State-sponsored messaging and censorship without revealing their identities or agenda. Now they'd be responsible for transporting the children away from the group homes and into nearby free zone refuges. The youngest ones would be taken to The Valley. Older ones would go to similar areas outside the main population. All would be adopted by willing families and begin learning how to live with their Psy abilities. They would be taught discipline, self-reliance, and charity. The protests organized by the religious leaders and the chaos caused by the tech guys would provide cover for the teachers to move.

After one of the bouncers was set to escort Curtis and the two women to The Valley, Mick made one last call.

"Hey, Brian. Sorry to bother you, but I'm afraid it's time."

"Where's the boss man."

"Bug's got himself in the big jar. Pappa went to break it."

"I see. Well, be safe, and thanks for the call."

* * *

"IT'S TIME." Father Patrick looked at his secretary, Mrs. Lacey.

She dropped her pen and notebook. After a moment of stunned silence, she picked up the notebook and called the teachers.

He continued on to Larry. The older man with a pot belly and a head full of silver hair was leaning over the old computer.

"I have something special I need you to print tonight. Get together all the volunteers you can find. We need to distribute this to everyone we can."

"What is it?" Larry looked at the new document transfer icon blinking in the folder on his desktop.

"It's a copy of special instructions to be followed after tonight's sermon. Send out a flash church service text to all the parishioners. We need to get everyone here in the next hour. And instruct them to bring a friend. This is going to be big."

Father Patrick spent the next hour waiting. He didn't need to rehearse. He'd thought about what he would say a lot over the years, and he knew God would help him say what needed to be said to reach the most people. As he walked out into the church, he was heartened to see the pews filled for the first time in years. While there were always regular attendees and sporadic holiday visitors, numbers had declined since the Storm.

The building was worn. Paint was peeling. The carpet faded, and the front door creaked loudly. But it wasn't the building that made up the church, anyway. The people did, and even if the building was demolished tomorrow, the church would carry on in the form of its true body. Wherever they went, the church would go, as long as they continued to search for a truth higher than themselves. That in mind, he took to the lectern and began.

"Thank you all for coming out on such short notice." He looked out at the field of faces.

Some were old, but a good many were young. They wore formal and casual clothing. Some came with families, some alone. A few brought children. One child asked for a bottle, followed by a shush from his mother, and it made Father Patrick smile.

"The world will change tonight in dramatic ways not experienced since the Storm, and each of you must choose how you will react and adapt to these changes. Right now, people everywhere are being called to take off the bands and protest the censorship that has imprisoned us for so long. Tonight we learn that there is another way."

Gasps resounded from the crowd.

"I've spoken with many of you over the years. A common concern voiced has been the feeling that something was missing out of life. You say and do all the right things, but in the end, you live and die in the same little box. Nothing ever changes. Every day is just like the last. People used to travel, take in the beauty of the mountains, art in the museums, fine food. They craved new experiences, and the world was more than willing to provide them. People had dreams, aspirations, and hopes. They dreamed of being something, accomplishing things, and if life wasn't giving them what they wanted, they made changes to attain those goals. They may not have always been successful, but they tried. When was the last time you felt like that? When was the last time you felt alive?"

There was shuffling and a few mumbled their agreement.

"Some of you remember those times. For those who are too young to remember, you feel a void without knowing what you're missing. The truth is, we need a purpose. Today, we serve without purpose, exist without living, enjoy without feeling, and fear repercussions every time we speak our minds or go against the norm. We do this because it keeps us safe. That's what we're told. They say if you deviate from the plan, Psy violence will destroy us all, as it almost destroyed the previous generation. We've learned from their mistakes, and things are better now. Maybe they aren't perfect, but we do the best with what we have. They told us it was for our protection and we believed them. We gave up our freedom for the promise of safety. We gave up our freedom for a lie."

Now people were covertly looking around to see the reactions of others. The boy ran his toy race car up and down the side of his seat and his mother quieted him again.

"Throughout history, we've treated symptoms instead of causes. People are quick to blame external sources for their problems. We all do it. Maybe you blame a movie or game. Maybe you blame poor education or economics. Maybe it's poor nutrition and competition. Some people blame God. All these things ignore one simple fact. We have free will. We are responsible for our own actions. You can ban books and sports. You can arrest people for not wearing a band around their head, but what does that do? It doesn't change the hearts of men. Because of free will, sometimes bad things happen. But great things happen as well. Back in the days of high philosophy, Hobbes and Rousseau had opposing arguments on what our true natures were. Are we inherently selfish and only do the right thing when forced to do so by laws and social pressure. Or are we inherently good and become corrupted by our environment to do bad things? No matter which theory you believe, the solution is not more laws and controls. If we are one or the other, we're doomed. If we're born selfish, we must be controlled to protect us from ourselves. If we're born innocent and become evil through exposure to our environment, our environment must be controlled to protect us from the outside. Both schools of thought ignore the fact that the people creating the laws are also human, and are therefore still bound by the same judgments of human nature they place upon us.

But none of that matters, because the world is not black or white. It's a wide range of grays. If we were truly mindless beings acting only on instinct, our society wouldn't have existed as long as it has. The truth is, there are acts of selfishness and acts of selfless kindness. People are persuaded to behave good or bad to avoid or provoke certain outcomes, but we are more than that. We are human, and that means something."

Everyone focused on him. He could see the yearning and hopeful fear in their eyes. They wanted truth.

"Some will say to look at our crime rates to prove that the controls work in keeping us safer. But there's problem with that assertion. Psy crime never went down. It was silenced, not stopped. People who speak the truth are arrested. Even police were arrested to keep their secrets. Anyone who shows exceptional Psy ability is taken away and imprisoned. You've all heard the rumors at one time or another. Maybe you knew someone who disappeared. Maybe it was a friend or coworker. Maybe it was a relative. While the current trends in society have cut many social ties and connections, they couldn't disconnect us from all experience. We still feel a need to interact with other people. We still crave friendship and companionship. We still seek patterns and traditions that make us feel like a part of a community, even if it's only in sharing a meal with co-workers or going to clubs with friends.

"After the Storm, we faced an emergency, but not the one we thought. Psy wasn't a curse. It didn't cause our society to fall apart. We were already those people. The Psy Storm just revealed that to us. It was a gift meant to show us what was truly in our own hearts. Thoughts are just as important as actions, and both can hurt. We were given these abilities, not to fear or hide from them but to learn from them. Instead of accepting the demons we saw, we were meant to become more than what we were. We were meant to become stronger and closer as a people. But we were confused and afraid, and we let ourselves be led. We faltered, and that was our mistake. But we can make things right again. The key is and always has been freedom. Without freedom, life is meaningless. We're told that we can't live without the bands or censorship to protect us from our own violent urges. We have no self-control. We can't help ourselves. We are merely beings acting on instinct. We aren't even allowed to read old stories or watch old football or baseball games, because they say competition and injuries breed anger and Psy violence. At one time, families took their children to these games to bond and create memories. It was part of our traditions, our history. It brought us closer together and gave us something to unite behind with our friends and neighbors. All that was taken away by someone sitting at a desk, making decisions about what he or she thought was best for us."

Some of the older people shook their heads in disgust. The younger ones hid their eyes.

"I'm here today to tell you that in many places throughout the country, people are living and thriving without these shackles. In these communities, people live unchained and they aren't killing each other. They produce uncensored art and literature. They preserve the documents of the past by sharing, reading, and remembering. They tell stories of their ancestors, of love and hope. In these places, people are taught discipline. They're taught to take responsibility for their thoughts and actions, and in return, they're free. Free to determine their own path. Life could be like this for everyone. Will we allow ourselves to be who they tell us we are? Or will we become who we were meant to be? This is your chance to take control of your life. You can choose to live in the dark, grateful for the little bits of light you're given. Or you can choose to make your own light and experience the wonders this world holds for you."

There were hopeful grins around the congregation, and he

felt a level of excitement in the air he hadn't experienced in years.

"We have a chance now to learn from our history instead of ignoring and destroying it. We don't have to be the violent animals they think we are. Instead, we can vow to take control over our own lives. The future is in your hands. Will you accept the shackles of the past or forge a new path free of oppression? Everyone must make this decision on his or her own. That's what freedom is all about. Some will choose to remain in the dark. All we can do for them is to continue to thrive in the light and show them, by example, what they can do."

Father Patrick took off his inhibitor band and sighed as the people followed in removing theirs. Larry and Mrs. Lacey went to the ends of each row to hand out the papers.

"Take these papers and share them with everyone you see. On the back you'll find a map to every church, synagogue, and temple in the city." He took his own copy out. "Life and Liberty given by man can be taken by man. Freedom comes from Truth. Seek always the truth and you will find it. Do not accept the shackles of fear. There is another way. Remove your band and gather together with your brothers and sisters of the community, in peaceful protest. And for any who find themselves in need of help or guidance, seek out a house of worship. The holy men and women there will help you. Be safe and go in peace with God, for He is always with you. Amen."

13

Lexy looked ahead and contemplated taking the alleyways. The Fixton building was close, and she could cut a lot of time off the walk if she darted between the buildings. But there were indications of unsafe energy hidden within the shadows of those alleys. The streets weren't much better. A group of cackling un-banded den rats straddled metal railings and leaned over benches in front of a seedy club. They threw bits of food and called out insults to passersby. Each of them reached out with tendrils of Psy energy at anyone who passed within a dozen feet of them. Those wearing inhibitor bands walked by without a flinch. But anyone without a band who reacted to the touches, were pounced on by all members of the group. And if someone tried passing on the opposite side of the street, one of them would dart across and follow them until the victim found a building to duck into and hide.

Lexy strode down the street, with her head held high, appearing confident. She felt their touches across her skin but kept moving, careful not to react. The touches gripped her breasts and rubbed her legs. She felt touches elsewhere and ignored them all. As suddenly as the touches had begun, they ended. She took a breath and noticed a man fall into step beside her. He smiled and nodded his hat to her. His energy was subdued, barely visible. Then the pulse tendrils couldn't reach her anymore. They were blocked from coming within several feet of her.

"You're a Shield," Lexy said.

He put a hand on her shoulder and led her to a gas station on the corner, facing the street that ran perpendicular to the one with the loiterers. They couldn't see her there. He opened the door to the station and waited for her to enter. She read what energy of his she could see and felt no threat. While looking into the dim interior of the gas station, she felt another light being hidden by him and saw an older woman about the same age as her mother. She had light blond hair and wore a standard blue work shirt and denim pants stained with oil and grease. The woman wiped her hands on a wet wash rag and held out one in greeting. Lexy shook her hand and sat next to a wooden table with a chess board carved on top.

The man sat beside Lexy and moved one of the chess pieces. "Check."

The woman cursed and sat down, then studied the pieces. "My name is Tracy." She didn't look up from their game. "This is my brother Daniel."

"Thank you," Lexy said to Daniel.

"Not a problem. I'm just the Shield. Tracy's the one who saw you and thought you could use a hand."

"Couldn't let a young un-banded Reader like you face those guys alone." She winked.

"You're a Reader?"

The woman nodded. "What brings you here? Curiosity, or lost a bet?"

"A bet?"

"You'd be surprised how many of those come down here.

Dares and bets. That's how most of the regular den rats start out." She moved a piece on the chess board and smiled.

Daniel pushed one of his pieces to the side. "Check."

The woman cursed again. "Anyway, you didn't answer my question. Why would an un-banded Reader be walking so close to Fixton? Don't you know how dangerous that is?"

"No more dangerous than running a gas station near Fixton, I would think. Which makes me wonder why you would help me and risk exposing yourself?"

The woman looked at Lexy, examining her Psy energy. "Your energy looks a lot like someone I once knew. I guess I got nostalgic."

"Who?"

She looked down at her board. "Just someone I used to work with. But that was a lifetime ago."

Lexy looked around the old gas station and saw a dusty, faded photograph behind the counter. In it, Tracy stood with a man holding her around the waist. Beside them stood a girl and a small boy who could've been her brother. Lexy looked at the woman's face in the photo and then at her face today. There was something familiar in her. She looked a lot like a woman Lexy remembered seeing in one of her father's old police photos.

"You were on the Reader Force."

Tracy looked up.

"My father was Logan Smith."

"Yeah, I thought you might be his little girl. Look at you, all grown up. So I suppose you've finally come to break your old man out of jail."

Lexy felt the color drain from her face. She searched for some sign of her father but couldn't sense him.

"You didn't know?" the woman said. "Then what are you here for?"

Lexy turned her gaze to Jared's light.

"I see. You've got someone else in there, too. Well, I'm sorry for you. You'll never see either of them again." She looked back down at her game and moved a piece.

Her brother knocked over her king, in checkmate, and pushed away from the table. She stood and started cleaning the front counter. She wouldn't meet Lexy's eyes.

"What if you help me?"

"Why would I do that? I barely managed to avoid going there myself twenty years ago. I have no intention of changing that now."

"My father would help you if the roles were reversed."

"Girl, you didn't even know your father."

"Am I wrong?"

The woman was quiet.

Her brother stood and looked at her. "Haven't we been hiding long enough? This was never supposed to be forever. We were going to regroup and plan our next move. Christine and Bill never would've wanted us to waste our lives away in some gas station surrounded by filth. Look, you know I'll protect you as long as I'm able, but this isn't living. Even if we die helping her, at least it'll be better than this. At least we'll be doing something."

"Dammit, Danny, I should be the one protecting you, not the other way around." She threw her rag down and leaned her head down onto her hands, elbows bent on the counter.

Lexy felt a surge from Jared and saw that his light flared in pain. She doubled-over and clutched her stomach. This wasn't the first pain she'd felt from him, but this was the most severe. She imagined what the pain was like for him, and squeezed a tear out of her eye. She moved to the door and opened it.

"Where are you going?" the woman asked.

Lexy didn't turn to look at her. "I don't know your story. I don't know what you've been through or who you've lost. Lord knows I'm no one to lecture anyone on the decisions they've made in their life. Up until I met Jared, I was too afraid to take off my band, even in my own home. He freed me and showed me there was another way. And right now, I'm pretty sure they're killing him, so I have to go."

"Do you even have a plan, little girl?" Tracy came from around the counter and stood behind Lexy.

She turned to face the woman. "Not really?"

Tracy rolled her eyes. "Kids. Come on, Danny. Looks like we're going to Fixton."

* * *

COLD METAL HIT Jared's skin. The attacker took his time, switched between weapons when he got bored, and Jared eventually ceased reacting to the blows. Some were flat. Some riddled with protrusions, and others had sharp edges. He took many cuts across his arms and face. Then he was shocked by the blinding pain of a blade plunged into his leg. He collapsed and nearly lost control of his energy, but he couldn't pulse. That was what they wanted and he refused to give in to them.

Although his leg hurt more than anything he'd ever experienced, it wasn't a life-threatening injury. But he wasn't so sure about the next stab wound in his side. Jared collapsed and blacked out. It was difficult for him to tell how long he was out. He felt around and his fingers touched something wet and sticky. He smelled blood. He waited for the final blow that would end this, but it didn't come. The air conditioner kicked back on. He'd survived another attack.

Jared pulled the sheets from his bed and tore strips to tie around his side and leg. He managed to put enough pressure on the two injuries to stop the flow of blood. Then he leaned back against the bed and rested. He was exhausted, and the next attack would kill him if he didn't find some way to fight back. His mind wandered and he found it increasingly hard to focus on anything. His energy surged and he pulled it back. He had to maintain control.

* * *

AN EQUAL NUMBER IN. An equal number out. That was the only way to fool Val. They had to make the patterns look the same as a normal night. The guards always delivered food in two-man teams, and it wasn't difficult to trick them into coming inside the cell. It had been over ten years since the last escape attempt. No one expected that to change tonight. So Old Man faked a heart attack. It made sense for everyone to crowd around to see what was wrong. The guards weren't even worried when the prisoners surrounded them, and neither saw the hit that knocked him out.

They were careful not to pulse. She would sense that. But they still had their hands, and as former police officers, they all knew how to use them. Then the group dispersed, with the guards seated beside the wall. Logan and Old Man continued the food deliveries down the hall. Prisoners were separated by Psy ability type. Back when they were first imprisoned, they were more spread out. But now they were lumped together in group cells.

Logan and Old Man went to each cell and cautioned the men to wait until every cell was unlocked before trying to escape. The only way this could work was if everyone made a break for it at the same time. Any earlier in the day and they would risk running into other guards throughout the building. But this late at night, there weren't many people around.

Logan struggled against the urge to rush. He could sense Lexy getting close. He counted his steps and hers.

Old Man put a hand on his shoulder. "She'll be fine. We're all getting out of here tonight."

They continued down the hall until the last of the low-security cells was unlocked. From their cells, the men and women watched their progress, and when the last door was opened, they rushed out, into action. Each Reader sprinted to a cell, took charge of their predetermined group of prisoners, and led them in different directions. With a Reader to lead them, prisoners had a better chance of avoiding guards and getting out safely. Splitting up insured that at least some of them would make it out. There weren't enough guards to track all of them. After taking care of the low-security cells, Logan and Old Man split up and hurried to open the doors of the individual cells.

* * *

JARED FELT THE DOOR OPEN, but the wound in his side hurt too much to sit up. He groaned. This was it. He wouldn't survive another attack. Bracing for the first hit, he pulled in all his Psy energy, ready for one last blow at his attacker. It probably wouldn't be enough to save him, but he had to try something.

He was surprised to feel warmth instead. His skin tingled, muscles eased, and he wondered what could be causing this. Then he remembered what Lexy had said about the warmth of a person's Psy energy when they tried to comfort someone. Still, he held onto his reserved Psy energy just in case he was wrong.

Fingers touched the side of his head, and the helmet hissed upon release. Sounds and light assailed him. He squeezed his eyes shut and covered his ears. A hand touched his shoulder while another held his arm for support. Jared cracked his eyes to see a bearded older man wearing the same prisoner clothing he wore.

"I'm helping you escape," the man whispered.

Jared gave a weak nod and leaned against the man, accepting his help off the bed.

"Can you walk?"

Jared put some weight on his injured leg. Pain was all he

felt, but he gritted his teeth and managed a slow hobble, with the man's help. He said a silent prayer of thanks that he was stabbed in the same leg as the injured ankle so that at least he had one leg to support his weight. They shuffled into the hall, where emergency lights were blinking and people sprinted. He looked in the room next to his, but it was empty and the door was hanging open. The five people who'd been in there were now gone.

"You should get out of here before they catch you," Jared said.

The man chuckled. "Don't worry about me. As long as we can stay ahead of Val, we'll be fine."

"Who's Val?"

"A Reader with a sadistic streak, who loves to manipulate and control people."

"Ah, I believe we've met."

"You did. She's the one who ran your first test, with the people in the other room."

Jared stopped and looked at the man. "How do you know about that?"

"I watched the whole thing from my cell."

"You're a Reader?"

"I am. Now let's get moving. Guards are on their way up to this floor. We need to get to the stairwell, ahead of them. There's not a lot of time."

The man was right—there wasn't much time. Jared could feel Lexy closer than ever. He had to get to her before she got captured or hurt.

They made it to the stairs, but going down was a nightmare. Every step tore at Jared's side. He held on to the man and the rail, grunting. They came out on the next floor and headed to a small kitchen.

The man helped Jared slide down to the floor, and then he looked around. "They have a service elevator somewhere along that back wall, but I haven't seen them use it in a while. Stay here while I see if I can get it working. That's going to be our best bet to get you down to the ground floor."

Jared nodded and closed his eyes to shut out the pain.

"And stay conscious," the man said.

But Jared was already out.

14

Lights flashed throughout the building.

Lexy looked at Tracy and raised an eyebrow. "What's going on. I see people running on every floor."

"Looks like a prison break." Tracy's eyes were wide, her mouth agape. "Danny, pull back your shield some so that I can get a better look."

A rush of excited energy poured over Lexy. Still watching the movement all around, she focused on Jared. He was moving slow.

"Looks like each group has a Reader with them," Lexy said.

"Alright," Tracy said, "then I'm going to see about disabling the security system. That'll give them a better chance of slipping out ahead of the guards."

"The guards don't have any Readers?"

Tracy's face became steely. "They have one. After I cut the system, I'll take care of her. You just get to your friend."

They rushed off and Lexy searched for a path upstairs. While running up an empty stairwell, she couldn't hold back her excitement and nervousness as she reached Jared's floor. He was stationary. She looked around for anyone else in the vicinity, but there was no one. Spots of red trailed the floor. She sprinted and opened the door to a tiled room filled with metal food carts. Following the blood and Jared's Psy energy, she rushed to him. Blood covered his shirt and side, seeping through the makeshift bandage wrapped around his wound. His face was ashen gray. She pressed her hands to his side to try and stop the blood flow, but it was leaking out too fast. So she focused her Psy energy and pushed against his skin with her hands and mind until the wound closed. While keeping her mental pressure on his injury, she pulled off the useless bandages and looked for something to replace them. Grabbed a stack of hand towels from the counter, tied several of them together, and tied them over another towel wadded up over his injury. She caressed his face and tried not to cry. There were bruises all over his chest and another severe injury on his leg. She was afraid of what she would find on the rest of his body.

"Jared," she whispered.

He barely opened his eyes and they were glazed over as he stared at her. "Nice hat."

She gave a nervous laugh. "It's Kara's."

"What are you doing here?" His voice was cracked and raspy.

"I should think that would be obvious?"

"You need to get out of here before they catch you." He lifted a bloody hand to her cheek and rubbed it.

She reached up and covered his hand with hers. She couldn't stop the tears from rolling down her face.

He grinned, weakly. "You're stubborn."

"She always was."

Lexy jumped. A shadow moved. She concentrated on the faint swirling Psy energy around the hidden man. How could she let anyone sneak up on them? She glanced around for a weapon. Then the man stepped forward and her heart stopped.

"Father?"

The man smiled. His eyes glistened with unshed tears.

When Tracy had said he was here, she was too afraid to believe it could be true. After years of thinking he must be dead, here he stood in front of her.

Lexy felt a glow of Psy energy appear on their floor. Her father turned to look in that direction.

"What's wrong?" Jared asked.

"Someone just came up on the elevator," she said. "He's coming this way."

"Where?"

"Uh, maybe twenty feet away, down the middle of the hall."

Jared pulsed, but the energy went too far to the side and missed the man.

He grunted. "Show me where."

She stared at him before feeling his energy touch hers. She followed his lead and stretched her energy to merge with his. Then he pulsed again. She directed it to the person. The man fell on contact.

"What did you do to him?" she asked.

"I put pressure on a nerve in his neck. It's a trick I learned at my dad's club. It's complicated to do, though. Takes a lot of focus. I usually don't have the time to use it properly, and I've never tried it without being able to see the person."

"Then we'd better get moving," her father said, "because there are a half-dozen guards coming up the stairs." He hurried to Jared's side and helped him stand.

Lexy physically held up his other side while also giving him extra Psy support to keep his weight off the injured leg. Her father led them to an elevator hidden behind a panel in the wall. It was big enough to carry a metal cart and person, so she and Jared fit in easily, but three was stretching it. Before she could turn around, her father was closing the gate.

"What are you doing?" she said.

He looked at her through the grating. "Get down to the first floor and get out of the building. I'll find you." Then he pulled the gate closed and hit the button to send them down.

"Daddy!" she cried.

It was pitch black in the elevator, which shook and clanged as it went down. Jared slumped and she tightened her grip around him.

He gasped and coughed. "Watch... the ribs. One's cracked."

She clamped a hand over her mouth to keep from crying out loud. "How did they find you?"

"It was some jerks I threw out of the club last night. They threw a girl in front of a car. I had to pulse so that the driver wouldn't hit her. Then they knocked me out and left me for the police to find."

Lexy cupped his face and kissed him. She felt him flinch as he twisted to face her, but it didn't stop him from returning the kiss.

The elevator rattled as it came to a stop. Lexy pulled the gate to open it and then helped Jared into the room. She didn't sense anyone below them, so she was certain they were on the first floor. She slowly led him through the hall, but they only made it a short distance, when she stiffened at a rush of Psy energy thrust in their direction. She ducked them inside the nearest room, leaned Jared against a desk and sprinted over to lock the door. Then she pushed furniture in front of it. People called out from the hall and beat against the door, shaking the furniture. She put her weight against it and tried to look for another way out, but there were no windows or other doors.

"Lexy?" Jared said, weakly. "Did my dad come with you?"

"No," she grunted and pushed back against the door. "But I had Curtis tell him where I was going. Why?"

"I think I felt him looking for me just now."

Lexy looked around Jared and saw wisps of energy reaching out to him. After following it, she saw a man standing outside the building. He had a tremendous amount of energy and was casting light in every direction, as though searching for someone. Beside him was a smaller, hazy glow.

"I see him. He's with Brian. They're working their way through the crowd outside."

She slipped from a slam against the door. The chair beneath her broke and she tumbled to the floor. A large cabinet tipped over and would've landed on her if Jared hadn't grabbed it and held it in place. The rags on his side turned bright red. Lexy scrambled to stand and then pushed her weight against the cabinet.

"Can you let him know where we are?" she asked.

"No, I've never been able to contact my dad. I could try to reach Brian even if he has his shield up, but I can't do it without knowing where he is."

"What about like you did upstairs? I could help you."

"How far away is he?"

"A few hundred feet."

"I don't know. I've never done that far before, especially not through a shield. And I barely have any strength left. Besides, I can't convey messages. Even if you could help me reach him, I can't tell him where we are. We'll just have to find another way out."

"I have an idea." She joined her energy with his again and directed his toward his father and Brian. "Pulse."

He sent out a strong pulse and she directed it to Brian while focusing on her and Jared's location. Brian's light flared slightly, still obscured by his shielding, and their two lights began moving toward them.

"They got the message," she said.

A moment later she was blinded by heavy pulses from just outside their door. As the waves passed through the walls, it was like stepping into a storm. The beating stopped. All the guards she sensed collapsed. Screams and pleas for help echoed. The sounds became fainter as they were dragged down the hall and thrown into another room.

"It's clear." She leaned against the wall of furniture, dizzy.

His energy was so strong that it was all she could see.

"Jared?" a deep voice called.

"In here," Jared said. "I think you're overwhelming Lexy."

The energy pulled back and a rush of oxygen entered her lungs. While blinking out the afterimage, she blindly pushed the cabinets until the door was clear. His father cursed the moment he saw his son. Brian rushed in behind him and the two men carried Jared out into the hall. Lexy called out a warning as new guards approached. A pulse of energy shot out from his father and the guards collapsed into a wailing mass. Lexy looked into the pulse and saw spiders and snakes crawling all over the men.

She followed until they made it to the front door, then turned and looked back up into the building to the spot where she'd left her father. Based on the groupings of guards, she had a good idea where he was.

"Lexy?" Jared called.

She gave him a gentle pulse kiss and then looked at his father. "Take care of him." She turned and hustled back upstairs.

* * *

"Where's she going?" Traymore asked.

"After her father," Jared said, feeling more helpless than ever. "He was arrested over a decade ago and brought here. He must've sensed she was coming, because he helped me escape, and I'm pretty sure he had something to do with this entire prison break."

Prisoners were rushing past them, out into the streets and deeper into the city.

Traymore sighed and looked at Brian. Then he strode in to go after Lexy.

BRIAN LED Jared out to his father's car and laid him across the backseat as sirens blared in the background. "Hold tight. I'm getting you out of here."

"What about Lexy and Dad?"

"Jared," Brian looked back at him from the front seat, "if I don't get you to a doctor soon, you're going to bleed out in this car. So sit tight and conserve your strength. This is going to be a long night."

Brian cranked the car and pulled out and zoomed down the back streets. The bumps sent jarring pain through Jared's body, but he didn't complain. It wasn't safe to go down the wired roads.

"I'm surprised there aren't more police out around here," Jared said.

"You can thank your girlfriend for that. She had a ton of files from her work. We're talking every censored document since the Storm. They prove every cover-up and document every crime for the past thirty years. She gave it to your father, and he put the plan in motion."

Jared sat up and instantly regretted it. "The plan. You mean, it's happening? Now?"

"Yeah. And lay back down. Your dad figured it would be a good distraction to get you out. Just before I met up with him here, he got word that the last of the children were safe in their new homes."

Jared slowly lowered himself back to the seat and tried to wrap his mind around everything. In the end, he only worried about Lexy and his dad.

* * *

LEXY FELT HIM FOLLOW HER. While waiting at the top of the stairs, she looked down and fought feelings of relief and agitation. She would've felt better if Traymore had gone with Jared. As strong as he was, she knew he could protect his son. But she would also be a lot safer with him by her side. His presence meant her safety. His absence meant Jared's safety.

A wave of Psy energy came down the hall. A group of thirteen guards were searching the rooms one at a time. She didn't sense any Readers with them. In fact, nearly all the Readers were now out of the building. She could still vaguely sense Tracy and her brother somewhere on the next floor, where Lexy thought she'd find her father. Also on that floor was a strong Reader's energy not obscured by any Shields. But other than a few more guards on this floor and the next, she didn't see anyone else in the building. All of the Psy signatures she'd felt inside earlier were now spread down the surrounding streets.

"How many?" Jared's father came up behind her.

"Baker's dozen. It's a tight group about twenty to thirty feet down the hall, to the right. Can you hit them with that spider hallucination trick you did downstairs?"

"You could see what I did?"

"I saw it on the pulse. I just don't understand how you did it."

"It's a manipulation of the electrical waves in their brains. I can modify what they see and hear. Then I throw in some light touches to strengthen the images their brain is sending them. But I can't do it without seeing them, and I can't do that many at once."

"I can see them. If you send your pulse, I might be able to direct it. I've done that with Jared twice tonight."

"Alright, then it's worth a try. Show me what you can do."

He sent out the pulse wave and she grabbed the energy and focused it on each of the guards. The first wave grabbed five people. He sent out another two pulses and she directed it to the remaining men. Though they were moving, she still hit her target. Stray images found their way into her own electrical currents, but she ignored them. She wouldn't let herself be afraid.

More overwhelming than the fear was her proximity to his pulse attacks. What it lacked in subtlety and finesse, it made up for with raw power. She swayed and would've fallen, but he put a hand on her shoulder to keep her standing.

"Are there more?" he asked.

She shook her head. "Everyone else is on the next floor. But they have a Reader by their side, so we won't be able to hide."

"Is your father up there?"

"I think so."

"Alright, then let's go get him."

* * *

THE ROOM WAS DARK. Blue emergency lights cast an eerie glow. They threw a smoke bomb into the auditorium, obscuring even more from view. Logan could still see where each of them were standing, but he couldn't see the furniture and fixtures. He felt her walk into the room and had to hold back his rage.

"Logan," she called. "I don't know what you hope to accomplish. You're outnumbered. Your friends will be rounded up and brought back. Security will be tightened and you will all take part in our next round of tests, as punishment for your disobedience."

"If that were true, you'd already have reinforcements here. There's something going on out there. I know you see it, too. The Psy energy in the cities is growing stronger. People are removing their bands. They've stopped listening to you and your bosses."

There were mumbles and rustling of feet.

"It's the beginning of a new world you don't control out there," Logan said.

"There will always be a need for control, and I'm well suited to that task. Things will go back to normal shortly."

"I wouldn't be so sure about that."

Tentacles of light reached up through the stairwell and invaded the minds of the guards. They collapsed on the floor, groaning and murmuring. Logan dashed for the door. Shots fired from across the room and bullets whirled through the smoke. He dropped and let them sail over his head. They slammed into the wall. She continued to blast off. Then Logan felt a flash of Psy energy behind Val. She stopped firing. Through the dispersing smoke, he saw her turn and look down the barrel of a gun aimed right at her face. For the first time he could remember, the cold mask of her face cracked. At the other end of the gun was Tracy Lin. Beside her, still masking their presence, was her brother.

"Hello, partner," Tracy said.

Logan came around the room so that he could see them more clearly. The women stood ten feet apart. Just enough distance to ensure Val couldn't pulse or attempt to disarm her. Should she try, Tracy's brother also carried a gun.

The fear left Val's face and she smiled. "Hello, Tracy. How's the family?"

Tracy's eye twitched, but her hand remained steady. "I'd say you could ask them, but you aren't going to the same place."

"How sad. After claiming you weren't a murderer, you're going to finally prove me right. I guess that means you won't get to see them either."

"You're the murderer. This is justice."

"Well, there's the charge, but I don't see a jury and I haven't been read my rights, so I'm afraid your claims of justice are faulty."

"What rights did you give my husband when you strangled

him in the pool? Or how about when you stabbed my sister in the head?"

"I never touched your husband, and it's not my fault if you and your sister didn't get along. After all, out of the two of us, you're the only one who could have TK'd your husband. Too bad you couldn't thought kill your sister, what with the block and all. So you had to default to a more rudimentary weapon, such as your handy kitchen knife."

Tracy bored holes into Val with her glare. "Stop the bull. We both know you can pulse and read. You killed my husband and sister and framed me for the crimes because I wouldn't help you set up the other guys on the force. I was your proof that everyone was at risk of snapping and becoming a danger to the public safety."

"Still delusional I see. Killing your family was too much for you to handle, so you had to invent a story with me as the bad guy. I understand. Really, I do. Come with me and we can get you the help you need."

"The only help I need is burying your body where no one will ever find it."

Lexy came out from the stairwell and walked over to Tracy's other side. She was followed by an older man who looked a lot like the injured man she came to rescue. His energy was similar as well.

"There's another option," the man said. "Put her on trial. Giver her that jury she asked for."

Tracy scoffed. "No judge will hear this case. She's too powerful, and they can't let the public know their secrets, all the crimes that've been covered up. It will never go to court."

"Yesterday, you would've been right. But today isn't yesterday. A little over an hour ago, every censored document and covered-up crime was released to the public. We paid special attention to the police departments, making sure each of them received a list of all the officers who've been wrongfully imprisoned over the past two decades. People are learning that they were lied to."

"That's impossible," Val said.

"Not if you work for History Remembered, like I do," Lexy said.

Val paled. "There's no way you could distribute all that information before it can be scrubbed."

"It's already out," the man said. "We printed it directly to the homes and distributed it through the churches."

The man dismissed the guards on the floor. They looked at each other and then at Val. Stood and hurried out of the room. Val pulled in her energy and pulsed toward Tracy. Before it could touch her, the man sent out a pulse that hit Val in the chest. The blow sent her to her knees and left her choking and gasping. Logan thought he heard a few bones break. Tracy forced Val to her feet and pushed her from the room.

"How did you know she was about to attack?" Lexy asked the man.

"I saw the way the three of you tensed and figured she was about to try something."

Lexy looked over at the man and sighed. A tear caught at the corner of her eye, and then she threw herself into her father's waiting arms.

15

There was a cool breeze as crickets chirped and rain tapped against the roof. Jared took a deep breath and cringed at the stiffness in his side. There were fresh bandages around his waist. From the pull of his skin, he guessed he had stitches. He opened his eyes. It was nighttime, but he was grateful not to be in complete darkness and silence. Under his back was the not so soft cushion of a real bed. He closed his eyes and tried to recall getting here, but all he could remember was the bumpy car ride and excruciating pain.

His Psy energy surged and he tried to pull it back, but his mind was blurred from medication and exhaustion. There wasn't any intention behind his pulsing and he couldn't tell if he was hitting anyone or not. People unlucky enough to be caught around him when he was like this usually felt they were being repeatedly punched or bumped. Once, when he was younger, he knocked a doctor unconscious for several minutes. While fighting to keep his eyes open, he prayed there was no one around to get hurt.

* * *

LEXY ROUSED when the car hit a deep pothole. Jared's dad was driving. She was in the backseat, her head rested against her father's chest and his arm wrapped around her. The intensity of her senses had dimmed from earlier. She couldn't see as far as before, at least not without extreme focus. But she also wasn't overwhelmed by the bombardment of sensations, as she'd expected with all the people removing their bands. It felt natural.

She looked out the window with her eyes and senses. She could see the outskirts of her city, but they weren't going there. From a quick glance at the roads, she could tell they were headed toward The Valley. It would be the safest place for them to recover. She wondered how Jared was and searched for his light. It was barely visible, hidden behind a hazy glow.

They drove down the service roads and she looked at the bright lights of a group of un-banded people sitting around a water fountain. Others approached and removed their bands, adding their glow as they sat among the group. Similar light groups gathered around the city in other central locations. All the Bands Offs demonstrations took place in restricted areas where band use was mandatory.

"Have you heard anything about Jared?" she asked Traymore.

He shook his head. "Phone lines are down. We expected as much. From the last report I got, phone calls demanding answers from the media, police, and politicians were clogging the system. Then all the lines went down."

"Cutting the phone lines is the first thing you want to do if you're trying to limit the spread of information," her father said.

"Only, they can't limit it," Jared's father said. "We've had this in the works for a long time."

He drove them through a back entrance to The Valley,

which led to the back of a large warehouse. Inside, Lexy saw several people she recognized and many she hadn't seen before. Mick was there with Curtis and Kara. Her mother sat, chatting with an older woman in a rocking chair. No sign of Jared or Brian, and Jared's Psy signature was difficult to read.

Her mother looked up and her mouth dropped. She stared at Logan with wide eyes. Lexy stepped back as her parent's rushed to each other. Their energies flared and surrounded each other. Lexy beamed as she watched them.

Her mom's eyes grew wide again as she peered over Logan's shoulder, at their daughter, and Kara jumped out of her seat, knocking over the chair. She rushed over and checked Lexy for any injuries.

"I'm fine. I know it looks bad, but it's not my blood. Where's Jared?"

"I'll take you to him." Paul led her and Jared's father from the warehouse to a small infirmary attached to the meditation instruction center. "He was in a lot of pain, so we had to sedate him. Of course, he has much greater control over his abilities when in pain than when drugged, so we've had to pull every Shield in The Valley to take positions in the medical center.

There were Shields everywhere. Young and old, men and women. The stronger ones walked around. Weaker ones stayed closer to the infirmary's closed door. With every step toward Jared, her senses dimmed. Lights winked out of her perception until all she could see was the glow of the shields created by Paul, Jared, and his father. Paul remained outside as they walked through the crystal-encrusted door. Lexy blinked as pulses shot across the room, bounced off the crystaled walls and shield fields. Ribbons of color swirled and combined. Light sparked and flared.

Jared's father moved to the bed and grabbed his son's hand. A pulse shot through Lexy and she gasped. She felt his touch on her skin. It lingered as though he was directing it, but his eyes remained closed. His breathing was deep.

"Are you alright?" his dad asked.

Lexy nodded and went to the other side of the bed. "There's just a lot of Psy energy in here."

She took Jared's other hand and sat.

"It'll get worse when he wakes up. At least, as long as he's medicated. You know, you look like crap."

She grinned. "Nothing a shower and a change of clothes won't fix."

"He'll be worried about you if he wakes up and sees you like this. Why don't you go get cleaned up and grab something to eat. I'll sit with him until you get back."

She stood, reluctantly. "You know, I just realized I haven't introduced myself. I'm Lexy."

"Traymore," he smiled. "Now go."

Paul showed her to a room and then brought her a white blouse and long brown skirt to change into. It wasn't her usual style, but she it would feel good to be in clean clothes again.

After she showered, she was admiring her loose hair and how good it felt to brush her hair without having to avoid an inhibitor band, when a crash echoed from down in the hall. A pulse of Psy energy shot from Jared's room, and a Shield was knocked down. She ran to Jared and dashed through the door. He groaned and writhed against the bed, his forehead wrinkled. She saw his energy pull in and shoot back out again. Paul, Traymore, and a doctor were leaning over the bed, trying to calm him down. Lexy pushed beside Paul and touched Jared's arm. She joined her Psy energy to his, and her vision exploded into light. Her body shook. Every nerve ending buzzed and tingled until her fingers went numb. She focused on his energy and directed it away from other people. What energy remained in the room, she split between the two of them.

Time disintegrated. His grip tightened around her hand,

and she put her head on his chest. Her knees slid down to the floor. With his other hand, he threaded his fingers through her hair and clutching at her scalp. She closed her eyes and listened to his heartbeat slow down. She heard the doctor move around and check the IV.

"I've increased the pain medication slightly, but I can increase it more if you need me to." His voice sounded far away.

Jared grunted.

"I know how much you hate it," the doctor said, "but I also know how much pain you've got to be in. Between that rib, your two stab wounds, and the multiple fractures in your foot, you're going to be out of commission for a while. If you need help, ask for it. We'll move you out to the treehouse if we have to. I just need you here until we're sure you won't need any more blood transfusions. I don't have the equipment out there for that."

"I'm fine," Jared said.

"Call me if he needs anything," the doctor said to Traymore and Paul.

"Lexy, do you need anything?" Paul whispered.

She shook her head. "I'm fine."

"Well, if you need anything let us know," Paul said. "I'll have someone outside all night."

She heard footsteps, and then the door closed. She saw the haze of the many Shields disperse, though they didn't go far.

"Lexy?" Jared's whispered.

"I'm here."

"You should go. I don't want to hurt you." His voice caught. "I can't focus while I'm on these drugs."

"I know. It's okay. I got you covered. I'll be your focus for now, like we did before."

Blue light surrounded them, and Lexy felt warm all the way through.

"I love you," she heard, through the pulse.

"I saw you," he said. "In the prison, in the darkness, I saw a light and knew it was you. You're all I saw. Did you find your father?"

"He's with my mother." She grinned. "What did my light look like?"

"Beautiful. I love you, Lexy. I want to marry you and have a real life together."

She looked up and stared into his eyes. "I want that, too."

Jared smiled, and she felt psychic lips touch hers.

"Good, I'm glad we got that settled." He put his head back down and closed his eyes. "I love you, Lexy," he repeated.

"I love you, too." Lexy put her head back on his chest and hugged him as tight as his injuries would allow.

* * *

IT WAS three days before Jared was strong enough to control his energy. In that time, she rarely left his side. The doctor changed the bandages daily. Brian brought the baby for visits, and Curtis brought Kara to announce their engagement. Lexy's parents checked in on them every day, but her father had a lot of his own healing and adjusting to do. And even with Lexy helping to focus Jared's Psy energy, it was a lot for her father to be around for long periods.

Traymore visited the most, a few times a day. He brought food and gave them updates from the outside world.

Protests continued. A special vote had been called to repeal all laws pertaining to inhibitor band use and censorship practices. Val's trial was scheduled for some time in the winter, and all the escaped prisoners had made it to The Valley or other sanctuaries.

When Jared was strong enough to leave the room, they were greeted with a feast that doubled as an engagement party and a welcome dinner for all the children brought into The Valley. As children played, Lexy sat by the man she loved while watching her parents dance.

"This is perfect," she said.

"Yes, it is," Jared said, from behind her.

Lexy turned and her mouth was captured in a passionate kiss. She felt a twinge of Psy energy deep in her belly and knew how perfect life could be.

ABOUT THE AUTHOR

"What do you want to be?"

When I was little, I answered that question with actor, writer, artist, astronaut, singer, fashion designer, and a few other things. Adults would grin at my answer and say I hadn't made up my mind yet. I told them, "No, I want to be all of them." I never understood the idea of limiting yourself to one thing. Life is so big. There's room for many adventures.

As I grew, I continued to draw. I wrote and performed songs at talent shows. I drew designs for clothing and even sewed some outfits. I made my own wedding dress, by hand. I studied digital design and learned to do some basic work in photo programs. My friends will tell you, I'm always jumping from one crazy project to another.

Again and again, I've been told what I was doing was too difficult, I didn't know enough, I could never do it. And every time, I've plunged headfirst into whatever my passion was driving me towards, with unwavering faith that I could do anything I put my mind to. People always want to tell you what you can't do. We're all capable of incredible things when we have faith and believe in ourselves. You may not succeed at everything you do, but you will never succeed at something you don't try.

Despite my vast array of interests, writing has long held a special place in my soul. When I was twelve years old, I spent an entire summer writing a story. Before that, I often started projects without finishing them. But this was different. I wrote every day. I wrote in the car, my room, and the laundromat. I wrote until my story was done. Just as vacation was coming to an end, I finished it, and. I knew in that moment this was my calling in life. This was what I was meant to do. From then on, I studied and wrote. Teachers and siblings told me to pursue a more practical career. I ignored them and followed my instincts. When I needed a break, I still had all my other creative projects to help me recharge. But I always returned to writing.

Through college, meeting and marrying my soulmate, working jobs I hated, becoming a mother to three wonderful boys, and homeschooling those same rambunctious boys, there have been challenges. There were times I've had to take a break from writing regularly to care for newborns and sick children. Though, even when I wasn't actively putting pen to paper—yes, I still use good old-fashioned notebooks much of the time—my books are always in my mind. I've spent many nights crouched over paper, using the dim light from my phone or a night light to see just enough to put down my thoughts, while my children sleep a few feet away. Writing is who I am.

My passion is paranormal romance and fantasy. I love writing about werewolves and other shapeshifters. I've also written about psychics. I began writing fantasy after I was married. My husband and I used to get together with friends to play dungeons and dragons every Saturday. He wanted to create his own world with his own campaigns, so he enlisted my help in writing the background stories. He described his world, the key players and asked me to write backgrounds on other characters. I would told him what I had, and he made changes to fit his vision. It was a lot of fun to work on this with him.

Later, I was looking for a quick project to write for NaNoW-riMo (national novel writing month) and decided transform our notes into a full story of its own. That was the birth of our first collaborative fantasy book project. It's great to be able to share something that's such a big part of my soul with my husband. He has always supported my writing. Even when it hasn't paid off financially, he's never once asked me to stop.

I don't know what the future holds, but I know this is what I'm called to do.

Psy Touch
ISBN: 978-4-86747-964-3

Published by
Next Chapter
1-60-20 Minami-Otsuka
170-0005 Toshima-Ku, Tokyo
+818035793528

30th May 2021